PUFFIN BOOKS

Killer Mushrooms Ate My Gran

Susan Gates was born in Grimsby. Her father was a guitar player and her mother a tailoress. At secondary school her favourite reading was science fiction – she read every science-fiction book in Cleethorpes public library. She also had a craze for all kinds of American literature, especially detective stories, and went on to study American literature at Warwick University. Then she became a teacher. She taught in Malawi, Africa (she still has a scar on her ankle from a mosquito bite that went septic), and in County Durham, England. She has three adorable teenage children (she has to say that – they might read this book!) Laura, Alex and Chris.

Some other books by Susan Gates

REVENGE OF THE TOFFEE MONSTER
ATTACK OF THE TENTACLED TERROR

Susan Gates

Killer Mushrooms Ate My Gran

PUFFIN BOOKS

PUFFIN BOOKS

Published by the Penguin Group
Penguin Books Ltd, 80 Strand, London WC2R 0RL, England
Penguin Putnam Inc., 375 Hudson Street, New York, New York 10014, USA
Penguin Books Australia Ltd, 250 Camberwell Road, Camberwell, Victoria 3124, Australia
Penguin Books Canada Ltd, 10 Alcorn Avenue, Toronto, Ontario, Canada M4V 3B2
Penguin Books India (P) Ltd, 11 Community Centre, Panchsheel Park, New Delhi – 110 017, India
Penguin Books (NZ) Ltd, Cnr Rosedale and Airborne Roads, Albany, Auckland, New Zealand
Penguin Books (South Africa) (Pty) Ltd, 24 Sturdee Avenue, Rosebank 2196, South Africa

Penguin Books Ltd, Registered Offices: 80 Strand, London WC2R 0RL, England

www.penguin.com

First published 2000
16

Text copyright © Susan Gates, 2000
All rights reserved

The moral right of the author has been asserted

Set in 14/17pt Baskerville

Made and printed in England by Clays Ltd, St Ives plc

British Library Cataloguing in Publication Data
A CIP catalogue record for this book is available from the British Library

ISBN 0-141-30526-6

Chapter One

When Maggot arrived at Gran's house, she was trying to read a mushroom.

She'd taken it out of a blue plastic box full of other button mushrooms.

Gran squinted at the mushroom. 'What's it say? I can't see without my specs.'

Maggot peered at the top of the mushroom. It had two words carved into it. He read them out loud: 'SAVE ME'.

Gran was already rummaging in the box. 'There's something written on this one too.'

She ran into the other room and came back with her reading glasses.

'This one says "HELP ME",' said Gran, in a puzzled voice. She handed it to Maggot.

'There's a face on it!' said Maggot.

I

Above the words 'HELP ME' someone had carved a tragic little face. It was like a sad clown. It had a turned-down mouth and tears squirting from its eyes.

'*Awww*,' said Maggot. 'It's crying. Are there any more mushrooms in there?' he asked Gran. 'With stuff written on them?'

Maggot tipped the mushrooms out on the kitchen table. A strong mouldy smell made him sneeze, '*Atchoo!*'

'Hey, how old are these mushrooms, Gran?' Instead of being white and plump, the tops were grey and wrinkly like elephant skin. '*Phew*, they stink.'

'I've had them since last week,' said Gran. 'But I only noticed the writing just now.' She rolled a few mushrooms over. 'There's nothing written on the rest,' she said.

'What's going on, Gran?' asked Maggot, completely baffled. 'Where'd those mushrooms come from?'

Gran showed him the empty blue box. It had 'JACK DASH. MUSHROOMS R ME.' written on the side in white letters. 'They were grown on a mushroom farm,' she said.

'A mushroom farm? Where is it?' asked Maggot. 'Is it near?'

'It's way out in the pea fields,' said Gran. 'The place that used to be an air base in World War Two.'

'Oh, that place!' said Maggot, feeling an instant cold shiver tickle his spine. 'Isn't there some kind of *scary story* about that place?'

'My gentleman-friend lives there,' Gran interrupted him. 'That's his name on the box. Jack Dash. He bought the mushroom farm last Christmas.'

'Oh right,' said Maggot slowly. He felt himself blushing. He knew Gran had a gentleman-friend. All the family knew. And they all agreed it was a *good thing*. Maggot's mum said: 'Your gran's been on her own since Grandpa died. That's years ago now! It's great for her to have some company. And she lives in such a lonely place. I wish she'd move into town, near us.'

It *was* lonely where Gran lived. There was a village near by. But her house was surrounded by fields, miles of flat, green, pea fields that stretched away in every direction.

She wouldn't move into town, where Maggot lived, no matter how much the family nagged her.

'She's so stubborn, your gran,' Maggot's mum had said, shaking her head.

Maggot had never talked to Gran about her gentleman-friend. He thought it was none of his business. And anyway, it was embarrassing, two wrinklies finding romance.

His cousin Emma had said, 'Gran's got a boyfriend. Isn't that sweet?'

But Maggot had shuddered. 'It's gross! What's she want a boyfriend for at her age?'

He frowned, reading the words on the mushrooms again. Whoever had carved them was in some kind of trouble.

'Do you think your – your *friend* wrote these?' he asked Gran awkwardly.

Gran sighed. 'I don't know,' she said. 'He's disappeared, Maggot. That's all I know.'

Maggot knew Gran was upset because she'd just called him Maggot. She hated that name. She didn't call him by his proper

4

name, Timothy, because she hated that too. She called him 'my flower'. Most other folk, even Mum, called him Maggot. It had been his name since he was two days old when he came home from hospital – a white, skinny, squirmy thing – and his brother Nigel had said, '*Uggh*, he looks like a maggot.'

Strangely, Maggot didn't mind his nickname. He didn't feel insulted. He was so used to it now that he never thought twice about it. Sometimes, when his teacher called out 'Timothy!' he'd look round the class and think, 'Who?' Besides, he might have felt left out without a nickname. Most of his friends had one. His best friend was called Spud because he had a head shaped like a potato.

Seeing Gran upset made Maggot upset too. He'd never known her like this before. 'Tell me what's up, Gran,' he begged her.

Gran dried her eyes. 'Well,' she said, sniffing bravely, 'Jack had been away, you see, on one of his plant-collecting trips.' She smiled shakily. 'What a mad, reckless daredevil he is! He nearly lost his life *again* this time. That man has got more lives than a cat –'

'Hang on,' interrupted Maggot, creasing up his face to show that he'd lost the plot. 'Who are we talking about?' He'd never met Gran's friend. But he had a picture of him in his head. A baldy old bloke shuffling about in carpet slippers who liked reading the papers and playing golf and pottering in the garden.

'My gentleman-friend, of course,' said Gran, sounding tetchy. 'Who do you think we're talking about? He's an amazing man, Jack Dash. He travels the world collecting plants. But his particular passion is collecting strange and exotic fungi, the stranger the better. He's brave, bold and fearless. Like Indiana Jones – only a botanist.'

'A daredevil *botanist*!' scoffed Maggot.

'And what's wrong with that?' demanded Gran. Maggot opened his mouth to make a smart remark, but Gran shot him such a fiery look that he clamped it shut again.

'He'll go anywhere to find a new fungus,' said Gran, warming to her story. 'To the most remote, most dangerous, war-torn corners of the planet. You've no idea of the hair-raising escapes he's had! Once he was cast adrift on a flimsy raft made of coconuts. He drifted for days and days, and only survived with the occasional snack of raw seagull and by drinking his own –'

'How disgusting!' cried Maggot.

'Yes, they would be a bit chewy,' admitted Gran.

'I'm not talking about the seagulls! I'm talking about drinking his own pee!'

'Nonsense,' said Gran briskly. 'You town kids are far too squeamish. Not like us country folk. Anyway, pee is very good for the complexion. Jack told me he had lovely skin, as soft as a baby's bottom, when he was picked up by that Chinese junk.'

'So this guy's some kind of hero then?' Maggot tried to sound sneery, but, secretly, he was rather impressed.

'You bet,' agreed Gran enthusiastically. 'You'd like him, I know you would. You two would get on like a house on fire. Anyway, Jack's last trip was to the jungle to collect a strange *giant* mushroom he'd heard about that grew there and nowhere else. Course, typical Jack, he got into some real scrapes. I mean, you should read his postcards! He got captured by fierce tribesmen who regarded the mushroom as sacred. But they were so impressed by Jack's lion-wrestling skills that they let him live and even made him an honorary prince of their tribe!'

'He wrestles lions?' marvelled Maggot, his eyes almost popping out of his head.

'Oh yes,' said Gran. 'He's a veteran lion-wrestler. He specially likes to wrestle the dangerous man-eating ones – he says it's more of a challenge. He wrestles grizzly bears too. And crocodiles, if they get too cheeky.'

'How old is this bloke?' asked Maggot, amazed.

'Oh, sixty-five next birthday. But you're only as old as you feel. Anyway, when Jack left for England, his new friends gave him three things. One was a royal spitting pot, the second some seeds from their sacred mushroom and the third was a special necklace to show he was a prince. And he promised them he'd wear the necklace always –'

Questions exploded from Maggot's mouth, he just couldn't stop them. 'Wow! A spitting pot! Was Jack good at spitting? I mean, was he a good shot? And what was the necklace like? Was it shrunken heads on a string? Lion's teeth? A monkey's claw?'

'Of course not.' Gran shook her head. 'The necklace was made out of bottle-tops. And very nice it looked too. Anyway, after that trip, Jack said he would settle down, stop his wild, wandering ways and become a mushroom farmer. We even planned to get married secretly –'

'What? Without telling Mum?' said Maggot, appalled.

'– and Jack had got a lovely suit, grey with a blue stripe. He hired it from Moss Bros. The full monty! Top hat and tails! We were going to be married last Wednesday.'

'So what happened?' asked Maggot.

'He didn't turn up, my flower,' said Gran, looking weepy again. 'I felt such an old fool! And I'd bought a lovely new hat as well.'

'Didn't he send you a note or anything?' said Maggot, outraged. 'What a creep! I hate him. Haven't you heard from him since?'

'Not a dicky bird,' said Gran, sadly. 'I cycled out to the mushroom farm on my racing bike and it was all locked up. His blue van was there, the one he used to deliver his mushrooms. But there was no sign of my Jack. No sign of life at all. The caravan he lives in was empty. I just found two lonely boxes of mushrooms left outside the gate. So I brought them home – for old time's sake.'

'And did the mushrooms in the other box have any messages written on them? Any cries for help or anything?'

'I don't know,' confessed Gran. 'I never looked. I ate them on toast.'

'You must hate that Jack!' said Maggot fiercely. 'Running off on your wedding day. Don't you hate him? I hate him!'

Gran gave a deep sigh. 'I don't *hate* him,' she said. 'I suppose he wasn't the type to get married. He was wild and free. Nothing could tie Jack down! Mushroom farming wasn't his style. I think he just got bored with button mushrooms. I'm not surprised. I mean, they're not exactly *interesting* are they? They all look the same, for a start. They must be the world's most boring fungi. No, strange and exotic fungi were Jack's thing. He's probably off somewhere now, in the foothills of the Himalayas, collecting some more of them.'

'So he didn't carve "SAVE ME" on this mushroom then? He didn't do this sad little face?'

'Who knows?' said Gran, with a sad little grin. 'Maybe it was a passionate cry for freedom. Like, "Save me from being a button mushroom farmer! Save me from getting married!"'

'Huh!' said Maggot. 'Funny thing to do, if you ask me. I mean, did he do that a lot? Write passionate things on mushrooms?'

'Not a lot,' said Gran looking misty-eyed and romantic. 'But he once bought me a box of mushrooms tied up with pink ribbon. And every mushroom had a little heart and my name "LILIAN" carved on it.'

Yurgh, thought Maggot, grimacing. I think I'm going to be sick.

'Anyway, he's gone now,' said Gran, giving herself a little shake like a wet dog.

'He's left everything behind – the mushroom farm, his van, *me* – so it doesn't matter, does it?'

But Maggot could see that his gran still had a soft spot for the wild and free lion-wrestling botanist, Jack Dash.

There was a long silence. In the middle of it, Maggot coughed like a barking seal: '*Arf, arf.*' He always did that when he was embarrassed. Then he thought of something to say: 'Can I borrow your racing bike, Gran? I just fancy a little ride round.'

To Maggot's relief, Gran seemed to be back to her old self. She had that fiery glint in her eye.

'Not before you take something for that wheezy cough of yours,' she said.

'Oh no,' groaned Maggot. 'Not one of your home-made remedies! No offence, but no thanks, Gran! My mum wouldn't like it.'

'Well, your mum's not here, is she?' snapped Gran, testily. Maggot's mum and Gran didn't get on all that well. They had very different ideas about bringing up children.

Gran was already thrusting a mug of

bright green, steaming liquid under Maggot's nose.

'*Awww*, Gran, have a heart! It smells like cheesy trainers! It looks like snot – or toxic waste or something!'

'What a fuss!' said Gran. 'It's a kind of herbal tea, a very ancient recipe. Jack brought the ingredients back from that last jungle trip. It's got dried tree bark in it and lots of other stuff. Jack said the entire tribe drank it all the time. Even the babies. And they were all fit as fleas.'

'Have *you* tried it then?' demanded Maggot.

'Er, no, I'm waiting until I get poorly, I don't want to waste it. But *you* can have some,' said Gran generously. 'It's a natural antibiotic, that is. It protects you from all sorts of nasty infections. It'll kill them all, stone dead.'

'Probably kill me as well,' grumbled Maggot. But it was a waste of time arguing with Gran – you always lost. So he held his nose and tipped the vile brew down his throat.

He had a violent shuddering fit. '*Urrgh*, that was *disgusting*!'

'Course it was,' said Gran coolly. 'That shows it's doing you good. By the way, my little flower, are you staying here tonight?'

Maggot often stayed at Gran's house. He hadn't been planning to stay tonight, he was supposed to go round to see Spud. But he thought Gran might need cheering up, so he changed his mind. 'OK,' he said. 'But I'll have to phone Mum.'

'I'll phone her now.'

While Gran was on the phone, Maggot slipped the two mushrooms, with their mysterious messages, into the pocket of his black, baggy pants. He didn't know why he did it. He just didn't want them thrown into the waste bin, that's all.

'Want my racing shorts?' enquired Gran, coming back from the phone. 'Get some sun on those pasty legs?' Gran's racing shorts were skin-tight, bright, ice-lolly orange and had 'N.E. LINCS ROAD RACING CLUB' written on them in sparkly gold letters.

'Er, no offence, but no thanks, Gran,' said

Maggot tactfully. 'I'd rather stick my head up a dinosaur's bottom than wear those shorts.'

Maggot cycled, in his old black baggies, along the yellow dirt tracks between the pea fields, He wasn't going anywhere in particular – just riding around. Just thinking. One of the things he thought was, Gran must be lonely, now Jack Dash has gone.

It made you feel lonely anyway, where Gran lived. All around Maggot were pea fields, nothing but flat, green, pea fields that seemed to go on for ever. The sky was like a massive blue bowl with just one white cloud loafing across. It made him feel very small, that sky – very small and insignificant.

He couldn't see any people anywhere. The only things moving, far out in the pea fields, were red metal monsters, like combine harvesters, that picked the peas. And lorries, that shuttled backwards and forwards, taking them to the frozen-food factory.

It was a very creepy place, like an alien planet where only machines could survive.

Then Maggot saw something else. What's

that over there? he thought, squinting over the pea fields at a brown smudge on the horizon. Are those buildings?

He gave a shiver of recognition. He knew what it was. It was the mushroom farm.

'What did you come out here for?' he asked himself, mystified. He always cycled in the other direction, towards the village. 'There's nothing interesting out here. No shops, no nothing.'

And he'd remembered that story now. He knew why the village kids never came near. They said the old air base was haunted: by a young airman who'd come limping home, in 1945, in a plane shot full of holes. He'd tried to land and didn't make it. His ghost still wandered round the place. That's what the village children said.

It's just a silly kids' story, thought Maggot scornfully.

All the same, he almost did a U-turn. But, suddenly, he felt those button mushrooms. They were bouncing around like jumping beans in his baggies. He pictured their pitiful appeals for help: 'Help me! Save me!'

And something made him carry on cycling towards the mushroom farm.

Chapter Two

Maggot laid Gran's racing bike down at the edge of a pea field.

He couldn't get into the mushroom farm because there was a high wire fence around it, with loops of barbed wire on top and a padlock and chain on the gate.

It looks like a fortress, he thought.

He didn't even go up to the fence. Instead, he crouched in the pea field, spying on the mushroom farm.

It seemed deserted. There was a row of long, low, wooden huts where airmen once lived. They were mushrooms sheds now, full of white button mushrooms. You couldn't see inside because the shed doors were closed and the windows boarded up. Mushrooms like to do their growing stealthily, in the dark.

There was a tiny caravan inside the fence and a blue van with 'JACK DASH. MUSH-ROOMS R ME' painted on the side. Maggot couldn't see a living soul anywhere. The mushroom farm was silent and still.

But Maggot didn't move from his hiding place. 'That's just a joke, that ghostly airman story,' he was telling himself. 'Just a little kid's spooky story. *Whoooo!* And anyway, everyone knows that ghosts only come out at night.'

But, somehow, he just couldn't get over the creepy feeling that he was being watched.

He shook off the feeling, 'Don't be stupid,' he told himself. 'There's no one in that mushroom farm. No one around for miles and miles.'

He strode out into the open, over to the fence. See, no one there, he reassured himself. But he still felt twitchy . . .

Hummmm.

What's that? thought Maggot. His head whipped round, startled by the sudden noise.

The hairs on the back of his neck were wriggling like icy worms. What's that?

He let out a long, '*Pheeew!*' of relief. 'They're only flies, you birdbrain,' he mocked himself. He could see them now. Fat, lazy bluebottles, swarms of them, buzzing about inside the fence.

That's a lot of flies, he thought vaguely. Then he forgot them as he moved along the fence to check out Jack Dash's caravan-home.

He could see right into it. There was no one there. Gran was right. Jack Dash had legged it.

He'd left lots of things behind though. The caravan was crammed full of stuff. Books mostly. Loads of books. And the ones he could see were all on one subject: fungi. Maggot had never seen so many books on mushrooms, toadstools, mildews and mould: *Fascinating Fungi*, *Fungi of the World*, *Deadly Poisonous Fungi*.

He certainly loved fungi, thought Maggot. The guy was a fungus freak. A lion-wrestling, pee-drinking, seagull-snacking, fungus freak.

Plus he was an honorary prince, Maggot reminded himself. Don't forget that.

You couldn't help being rather impressed by someone like that. Even if he did run out on your gran on her wedding day.

'Jack Dash could have been my new grandpa,' Maggot told himself, almost wistfully. Maggot didn't remember his old grandpa. He had died before Maggot was born.

Maggot climbed up the wire so he could see into the caravan more easily. And he spotted something on the floor. It was a strange little pot, about the size of a yoghurt pot. It was made of some silvery metal. It had a lid engraved with mysterious signs and symbols. Maggot guessed straightaway what it was.

'That's the royal spitting pot,' he murmured, in an awed voice. What did Jack Dash leave that behind for? It was a present from his friends. I'd have taken it with me, decided Maggot. I wouldn't have left it behind.

He'd seen everything to see in Jack's

caravan. He asked himself, 'What shall I do now?'

He thought briefly about trying to get inside the mushroom farm, about climbing the fence. He looked upwards. No way, he decided, shaking his head. That barbed wire looked cruel. It could shred you like coleslaw.

Maggot jumped down off the wire fence. He glanced at the sky. The weather was changing fast. The sky was filling with up storm clouds now, like black sheep piling into a blue meadow.

Where'd they come from? thought Maggot, alarmed.

Soon you couldn't see any blue at all. Then, *pop*, the sun vanished and the day was instantly dark as evening.

Maggot gazed through the fence at those low wooden sheds. He shivered. The place looked different now – sinister in the gloom. Like a prison camp. 'Time to go back to Gran's,' he told himself. 'Don't know why you came out here anyway.'

As he was turning to go, a flicker of movement caught his eye. He couldn't help looking. Something was creeping through the grey light, keeping close to the shed walls. A fuzzy pale shape. Was it a man? It glowed like the moon at night. Was it – ?

Maggot's face twisted in horror. It's the ghostly airman! his brain shrieked at him. RUN! RUN!

He raced away. But bounced back, *boing*, as if he was on elastic. His baggies were hooked on to the fence. He was trapped!

'Oh no! Oh no! Oh no!' Maggot gibbered, struggling frantically to escape.

His pocket ripped. The 'SAVE ME' mushroom spilled out on the grass. But Maggot didn't stop to pick it up. He was free! He panted back to the pea field, grabbed Gran's bike, hopped on and cycled away like a maniac. He didn't once look back.

As he rode, the storm broke with a great crack of thunder. Grey sheets of rain came hissing down. The dirt tracks turned into yellow rivers. By the time he reached Gran's, Maggot was wet through, like a great, soggy sponge that needs squeezing out.

'*Tut, tut,*' said Gran as he squelched

23

through the door and stood in a puddle. 'You're a trifle damp. I know what you need. I know what'll stop you getting pneumonia. A nice double dose of my special tea!'

Chapter Three

Yurgh! thought Maggot, making a hideous face.

That green tea taste really lingered on. As if he'd been sucking a festering sock.

At least he'd calmed down a bit. His heart had stopped rattling his ribs. And he was trying to tell Gran what had scared him so much.

'I saw the ghost of the airman, Gran. I really did! That story the village kids tell is true!'

But doubt was already creeping into his voice. Did I really see a ghost? he was wondering. He'd been half-hysterical; his memory was scrambled. That weird luminous shape – he'd only seen it for a second.

25

He could have made a mistake. It could have been phosphorescence, a stray lightning flash. Strange things happen in thunder storms.

In any case, Gran had no time for the village kids' story. She just said, in her down-to-earth way, 'It's a load of old twaddle. Whatever you saw, it wasn't a ghost.' And she sounded so sure, so one hundred per cent certain, that Maggot began to believe her.

What really got Gran fizzing with questions was what Maggot had seen in Jack Dash's caravan.

She asked him to describe the little metal pot. 'What did it look like?'

'Sort of silvery, with all these weird signs and things on it.'

'There's no doubt about it,' announced Gran. 'It's the royal spitting pot all right. I can't understand it. Jack really treasured that pot. Why didn't he take it with him?'

'I wondered that!' said Maggot, nodding.

'It contained something really precious,' said Gran. 'I can't believe he'd go anywhere without it.'

'What did it have in it?' asked Maggot, his eyes boggling. 'You're not telling me it had spit in it? No offence Gran, but that's disgusting. Even if it *is* a king's spit.'

'No, no,' said Gran. 'Don't be silly. It didn't have a king's spit in it. It didn't have anyone's spit in it. It was a *ceremonial* spitting pot. It probably hadn't been used for hundreds of years.'

'Oh, right,' said Maggot, feeling vaguely disappointed. He'd had some wild fantasies about that pot. He'd imagined a sort of royal spitting competition that anyone in the kingdom could enter. And the person with the longest spit and deadliest aim would get to be crowned king – or queen.

But Gran was asking him a question.

'Remember I told you that, along with the bottle-top necklace and the spitting pot, they gave Jack some spores – you know, the seeds of their sacred mushroom?'

Maggot nodded.

'Well,' continued Gran, 'Jack brought those spores back home in that spitting pot. He was going to try and grow the mushroom.

He said it was the weirdest fungus he'd ever seen. A real show-stopper. He was so excited about it. Wherever he went, that pot would go with him. I'm sure it would.'

Maggot felt confused. 'So what are you saying then, Gran? Did Jack Dash leg it on your wedding day, or what?'

'I *assumed* he did,' said Gran thoughtfully. 'I assumed he got itchy feet and set off. You know, to some distant shore, some forgotten part of the world. But maybe I assumed wrong. Maybe there's some other explanation.'

'What though?' asked Maggot, more confused than ever.

'I don't know,' answered Gran, in a grim voice. 'But I'll tell you what – you and me are going to go out to that mushroom farm tomorrow.'

'We can't get in,' explained Maggot. 'It's all locked up, isn't it? And there's this whopping big barbed-wire fence –'

'Oh, didn't I tell you?' said Gran. 'I've got a key. I could've let myself in last Wednesday. But I didn't. I just biked out there and saw Jack's caravan was empty and there was a padlock on the gate. And I thought, that's it then, Lilian, he's gone for good. I mean, I was a bit upset – and I had my flowery hat on and my wedding frock.'

'Course you were upset!' agreed Maggot loyally. 'But didn't you think it was strange that he'd left his van behind? That one with "MUSHROOMS R ME" on the side?'

'Actually,' said Gran, 'now you come to mention it, I did think that was a bit odd.'

'You sure you want to go out there, Gran?' asked Maggot. 'It might get you upset all over again.'

To be honest, it wasn't just Gran's feelings Maggot was worried about. It was his own too. That mushroom farm was a strange and spooky place. He could understand why the village kids never went near it. His heart began fluttering all over again. Thirty seconds ago he'd convinced himself that the ghostly airman didn't exist. But what if he was terribly wrong?

'Cos you've been terribly wrong before,' Maggot reminded himself, 'about all sorts of things. What about the time you thought they put teachers away in the school cupboards at night and wheeled them out in the morning? Or the time you thought Spud had a fatal disease because he was covered in big red spots? You said, Oh no, Spud's going to die! And he'd only been sunbathing in his mesh T-shirt? Or the time – ?' He could have gone on and on for hours, days.

But Gran was talking to him. 'Don't you worry about me,' she was saying, in her steeliest voice. 'I'll be fine. I just want to have a quick look inside. To settle my mind. You needn't come if you don't want to.'

'Course I'm coming,' said Maggot. 'You don't think I'm *scared*, do you?'

That night it took Maggot ages to get to sleep. And when he did sleep, Jack Dash and the ghostly airman got all tangled up in his dreams. The glowing ghost, still in its tattered World War Two flying suit, came springing at him like a lion. *Grrrr!* But Jack Dash wrestled the ghost and won!

'You saved me!' Maggot told Jack Dash, in his dreams.

'Oh, *pting*, it was nothing,' said Jack Dash, punctuating his answer by spitting neatly into the royal spitting pot. 'Nothing at all, *ptong*!'

Chapter Four

Gran hitched up her orange racing shorts. She pulled on her fingerless cycling gloves and fastened her red cycling helmet. On Gran's tiny head it looked like a giant wobbling strawberry.

She was ready for action. 'Let's go, my flower,' she said, in her most determined voice.

'OK, *ptong*!' said Maggot.

'Was that a cough?' asked Gran suspiciously.

'No, *pting*, it was a full stop,' Maggot tried to explain.

He hardly noticed that Gran was opening cupboards and mixing things. He was still thinking about his dream. He couldn't seem to get them out of his head – those lovely musical notes when Jack Dash's spit struck the metal pot, making it ring, *pting*, like a tiny gong. He found himself copying Jack Dash. Making *ptinging* and *ptonging* sounds every time he opened his mouth. He didn't actually *spit* though. Not in Gran's kitchen. Only someone with Jack Dash's style could get away with that.

'He was a brilliant shot,' murmured Maggot, in an awed voice. 'He never missed that royal spitting pot. Not once, *ptong*. How cool is that?'

But then he was forced to shake off last night's dream because Gran was approaching him, looking dangerous. She had a steaming mugful of her kill-or-cure medicine.

'Oh no!' groaned Maggot. His stomach cringed at the thought of that foul, bright green liquid.

But he glugged it down, just to keep the peace.

'*Ugghh!*' The tea slid down to his stomach and started a war with his cornflakes. 'Gran, are you sure this stuff is safe to drink?'

'I told you,' said Gran impatiently. 'It kills infections inside and out. That tribe, the one Jack was honorary prince of, even rubbed it on to kill foot fungus. You should try it. You've got that, haven't you, a horrible, white, smelly fungus between your toes? Your mum told me.'

'*Arf, arf,*' coughed Maggot, doing his seal act. Why did mums embarrass you so much? Blabbing your personal, private medical problems to other people?

'See,' said Gran. 'You've still got that cough. I knew it! Never mind, you can have another dose of tea tonight.'

Things got even more embarrassing. Instead of Gran's flash racing machine, Maggot was forced to ride her creaky old cycle. The one she'd used before she got keen on road racing. It had a basket in front for shopping. And very high handles that made you look like a begging dog on a bike.

Gran whizzed through the pea fields with Maggot bouncing along behind her.

At least none of my mates can see me,

thought Maggot gratefully. Nobody can see me out here.

They seemed to be the only human beings in the landscape. The pea fields spread out on either side, wide and empty as a green desert.

We're here, thought Maggot, feeling a familiar fluttering in his stomach.

He climbed off his bike. The mushroom farm looked just the same. Silent and still in the sunshine. Not even a breeze blew to stir up the dust.

And there isn't a ghost. That's a load of old twaddle, Maggot reassured himself. But there was still something menacing about the place. He looked nervously over his shoulder.

He remembered something. He reached into the ripped pocket of his baggies for the 'HELP ME' mushroom.

'*Euch!*' His hand came out covered in goo. The mushroom that was left had dissolved into sticky black slime.

He wiped his hand on his baggies. He tried to calm his twitchy nerves. But he couldn't help it. That tiny fluttering became wild beating wings. He suddenly felt a terrible sense of doom . . .

'Come on,' urged Gran, getting a key out her bumbag and unlocking the gate. 'Don't look so dozy! Let's go in and take a peek at this caravan.'

Maggot gulped down his fears and followed Gran into the mushroom farm.

Buzzzz! Fat blue flies dive-bombed their heads.

'Gerroff!' shouted Maggot, waving his arms like a windmill.

'Don't get your knickers in a twist,' said Gran, swatting them away. 'They're only flies. There are a lot of them though, aren't there? I wonder where they all come from?'

Gran strode purposefully past the boarded-up sheds.

She took another key out of her bumbag. But she didn't need it.

'Jack's caravan isn't even locked,' she said, surprised, pushing the door open.

Maggot climbed in after her. Nothing had been disturbed since he looked through the windows yesterday. All the books were in the same place and so was the spitting pot.

'There's the pot,' he said. He almost said, 'There's the pot, *ptong*!' but he stopped himself, just in time.

'That's it.' Gran sat down on the caravan floor and picked up the pot, very respectfully, in both hands. 'I don't understand Jack leaving this. Actually, I don't understand Jack abandoning his mushrooms either. That's not like him at all, even if they were just boring, old button mushrooms. '"Mushrooms need a lot of attention," Jack once said, They're like babies.'

'He must have known a lot about mushrooms,' said Maggot, sweeping his arms round Jack's fungus library, 'if he read all this lot.'

'Oh he did,' agreed Gran. 'He was a fungus expert. He had fungi on the brain. He taught me a lot about them too. They're fascinating things! Did you know, for example,' said Gran, 'that mushrooms aren't really plants. They're more closely related to animals. That means *you* are related to a mushroom.'

'You're kidding me!' said Maggot, horrified, thinking of the smelly black slime in his pocket.

'I'm afraid you are,' said Gran. 'Mushrooms are our cousins. They're practically family! They've got some of the same proteins as we do. I read about it in *New Scientist*. And you'd think mushrooms were slow, wouldn't you? But no! Some fungi are really fast movers! They sneak up on you. One day they're not there. The next day,' Gran snapped her fingers, 'there's a whole bunch of 'em! And another thing, they're strong as well. You wouldn't think that either. But when mushrooms grow they can push up paving stones! They're a very successful species. Like rats and cockroaches, they could probably take over the world!'

Oh no, thought Maggot, raising his eyebrows and sighing loudly. Gran's a fungus freak now.

'And *another* thing about fungi,' Gran was rabbiting on, 'some of them can glow in the dark. Did you know that? And the poisonous ones have great names like Death Cap and

Destroying Angel and Satan's Boletus. And did you realize–' But then she suddenly stopped dead. She'd lifted the lid off the spitting pot and was gazing into it with a startled look on her face.

'It's open!' she said. 'It's supposed to be sealed with beeswax to keep the spores safe inside.' She peered more closely into it. 'The seal is broken. The spores are gone,' she said. 'This pot is empty.'

'What spores?'

'You know, I told you, of the mushroom Jack brought back from his last trip. He didn't think it would grow here, he wasn't hopeful at all. But he wanted to try. He said it would be truly spectacular. He said just one look at it would blow your brains out!'

Maggot shrugged. 'What do mushroom spores look like?'

'Oh, nothing really. A sort of greyish, whitish powder.'

'Maybe they blew away. Or maybe Jack took the spores with him – and left the pot behind.'

'Maybe,' agreed Gran slowly. But

39

Maggot could see that she wasn't convinced.

Gran jumped up, as if she'd suddenly made a decision. She put the spitting pot on the table. 'I just want to check something,' she said.

'What? What do you want to check?' asked Maggot uneasily.

It wasn't just his own fears that were making him jumpy. He was scared for Gran as well. He thought that all these reminders of Jack Dash would make things more painful. He didn't want Gran hurt any more. He wanted to tell her, 'Jack Dash is probably thousands of miles away by now. In the jungle or up a mountain or somewhere. I don't think he's coming back, Gran. Forget him.'

But somehow he couldn't talk about the things that were troubling him. It was too embarrassing. So he barked, '*Arf, arf,*' and said, 'When are we going home?'

'Do stop moaning,' said Gran. 'We'll go in a minute. I just want a look in those mushrooms sheds. There's something wrong here. Something terribly wrong. I can smell it, my flower. I can feel it in my bones.'

Chapter Five

Gran went striding towards the mushroom sheds. It was hard to keep up with her. Her legs were strong and muscular from all that biking.

'Gran, wait for me!'

But before Maggot raced after her, he took the ceremonial spitting pot and stashed it carefully away in the knee-pocket of his baggies. It should be treated with respect. Not left behind for any kid to find.

They wouldn't realize what it was. They'd think it was just some trashy old thing. They might park their chewed gum in it. Or use it to store their toenail clippings! thought Maggot, appalled, as he jogged after his gran, with the royal pot clinking inside his trousers.

He was too slow. Gran had already disappeared into a shed. 'Which one?' thought Maggot, panicking.

Without thinking, he yanked open the door of the nearest shed and dived into it yelling, 'Gran? You in here?'

Blackness immediately swallowed him up. It was like going down a mine.

'Gran?'

No answer. He wrinkled his nose. There was a strong mouldy smell. The darkness reeked of old graveyards.

At first he couldn't make out anything at all. Gradually his eyes got used to the gloom.

Stacks of mushroom beds rose like shelves on each side of him. And, in each bed, button mushrooms were growing, crowds and crowds of them. It was like a strange supermarket that sold nothing but mushrooms. Everywhere you looked, smooth white tops swelled through compost, like thousands of tiny skulls.

Creepy, Maggot decided. He still felt jumpy. But he wasn't in a panic or anything. He wandered up and down a few aisles. There were no surprises. Nothing really threatening or dangerous. Just more and more button mushrooms. Round white mushroom heads all around him, above him. They seemed to be leaning over the edge of their mushroom beds, slyly watching him.

Without any warning, hairs began prickling on the back of his neck. He was remembering what Gran had said. 'Mushrooms sneak up on you.'

The place wasn't in total blackness. Tiny lights, small as Christmas tree lights, were clipped on to each mushroom bed. They were very dim, just bright enough for whoever was picking mushrooms to see what they were doing.

And someone *had* been picking mushrooms. He saw a blue box, half full. And a sharp mushroom-picker's knife lying on the compost, ready to slice off some more.

That knife, thought Maggot immediately, that could have been used to carve the messages on those mushrooms.

'Gran?' he called out again. His voice echoed eerily round the shed.

Everywhere he turned there were mushrooms and more mushrooms. Like a silent ghostly tribe, creeping up on him in the dark.

Suddenly he felt spooked. Got to get out of here!

He ran for the exit, with the royal spitting pot rattling in his baggies. He stumbled out into the fresh air.

'What did you run for?' he mocked himself, as he stood blinking in the sunshine. 'They were only mushrooms. They're probably more scared of you than you are of them! They were probably saying, "Oh no, look out, here's a human! Help, help! He'll eat us all up! He'll have us on toast!"'

His impression, in a high twittering voice, of frantic button mushrooms, sounded so silly that Maggot managed a weedy grin. It made him feel a bit better. He looked around. Still no sign of Gran. He batted a few flies away.

Where is she? he fretted. She must have gone into a different shed. Maybe the next shed along. He looked at it nervously.

'You should go in there,' he told himself.

But he didn't feel very thrilled about it. At the back of his mind, like a nasty itch, that ghostly airman was still bothering him.

He gave himself a little pep talk.

'You've got to find Gran,' he told himself sternly. 'And what are you scared of? If you go in there, what'll you find? Just millions of round white mushrooms. They all look the same – like *pting-ptong* balls! I mean ping-pong balls. And they haven't even got any interesting messages written on them. Yawn, yawn! Gran was right. Button mushrooms are the world's most boring fungi. You can't take them seriously, can you? I bet Jack Dash soon got fed up with 'em. You can't blame him. Not after the exciting life he's led.'

Maggot *did* blame Jack though, for running out on Gran on their wedding day. He shouldn't have done that, thought Maggot, for the hundredth time, as he pushed open the door of the second mushroom shed.

'Gran?'

Maggot had expected more neat little button mushrooms: all clean and white and blank, all looking exactly the same. He was in for a big shock.

First he saw what he thought were sombre jewels – rubies, emeralds, sapphires, in the dim glow of the mushroom-picker's lights. Then his eyes adjusted.

'*Wow*,' he breathed.

He'd never seen anything like it. He didn't know fungi this weird existed!

They were sneaking over the edge of the mushroom beds, pushing up through the floor, hanging anywhere they could get a grip. They had taken over the shed and driven out the button mushrooms. There wasn't a boring button mushroom in sight!

These fungi were all sizes, all shapes. From tiny toadstools to great big puffballs. They were all colours! From sickly yellow to poisonous blue. Those toadstools were black and rubbery like liquorice. That strange purple fungus was like a honeycomb. There was even an orange frilly fungus creeping across the shed roof. Fungus like dead grey fingers. Fungus flowing like white lava down the shed walls. Some were like soft jelly eggs, some were warty, some slimy. A crusty fungus, growing on wood, gave off an eerie green glow.

Maggot stared, half-revolted, half-fascinated, at that gruesome fungus garden.

'I know what this is,' he murmured. 'This is Jack Dash's exotic fungus collection.'

Only, since Jack left, it seemed to have got a little bit out of control . . .

What's that? thought Maggot. His head whipped round. He thought he'd heard a faint shuffling sound.

'*Aaaargh!*' Something grabbed him! Something sprang at him out of the dark. Thin white fingers like roots clutched his arms. They had incredible strength. A strong mouldy smell almost choked him. Maggot twisted round. A luminous face peered into his own. Its eyes had no colour. They were pale and shiny as pearls.

'Oh no,' Maggot's brain screamed at him, before it dissolved into total panic, 'it's the ghostly airman!'

'Gran! Gran!' he screamed, struggling madly.

But no one rushed to help him.

He kicked out frantically, but he was help-less. He felt himself clutched by rubbery octopus arms, almost lifted off his feet. He was dragged through a maze of dark aisles, swept along, he couldn't resist.

'Where are you taking me?' screamed Maggot.

But the Thing didn't answer. Maggot was hustled through a door. Then suddenly he was released. He dropped in a heap on the floor, squashing a cluster of crimson-streaked toadstools.

Maggot sprawled there, trembling. *Boom! Boom! Boom!* What was that racket? It was his own heart, trying to burst through his ribcage.

He lifted his head very slowly. The roaring in his ears died down.

The Thing had scuttled into a corner. Now, for the first time, he had a good look at it. It crouched there, slyly watching him. Its eyes glittered from under the brim of a strange, tall hat.

It was thin and spindly, like a seedling

grown in the dark. Its lips were like chalk. You could see its skin, as white and waxy as church candles, through its tattered clothes.

Hang on a mo! Maggot finally twigged. That's not a World War Two flying suit!

Along with the top hat, the Thing wore a tail coat and trousers. The whole outfit was speckled with rust and mildew. It seemed to be mouldering away. But you could see it had once been a really posh suit – grey, with a tasteful blue stripe.

'It's Jack's wedding suit,' gasped Maggot. Something jingled round the Thing's scrawny white neck. Bottle tops threaded on string . . .

'The honorary prince's necklace! The one Jack Dash said he would never, ever take off.'

Maggot got up, still feeling shaky. But he was more excited than scared. He took a few wobbly steps forward.

He held out his hand in greeting to the top-hatted ghoul.

'Jack Dash, I presume!' he said.

Chapter Six

Jack Dash didn't shake Maggot's hand. He didn't speak. He was as silent as a mushroom.

He didn't even seem to know his own name.

'You are Jack Dash, aren't you? The daredevil botanist?' Maggot tried again eagerly. 'The pee-drinking, seagull-snacking, wild adventurer?'

Jack Dash licked his dry lips with a white rubbery tongue. But the eyes didn't flicker. So Maggot introduced himself. 'I'm Maggot.' He coughed awkwardly, '*Arf! Arf!*' before he could continue. Then he said, 'You know, Lilian, your girlfriend, well, she's actually my gran – actually.'

There was no recognition on Jack's face. Or in those washed-out zombie eyes. This wasn't the handsome hero Gran had described. This freak hardly looked human at all!

A rogue thought went flashing through Maggot's mind. Maybe that's what happens to you when you drink your own pee.

Then he thought he glimpsed something, deep down. A spark of a human expression. Some kind of hopeless, pleading look on that deathly white face. It vanished as soon as he'd spotted it.

But Maggot had seen it. He was certain of it.

Feverishly he scrabbled in his baggies. He brought out the royal spitting pot. He held it out to Jack, like you hold out a lollipop to a baby.

'I bet you remember this, *ptong*!' he gabbled, desperate to make contact. 'You know, when you wrestled that man-eating lion and they gave you that bottle-top necklace and this pot with the mushroom spores inside?'

With chilling speed a white claw shot out.

It grabbed the pot in a vice-like grip and cuddled it. Then stuck it in the pocket of the wedding suit. 'Hey! You didn't have to snatch,' said Maggot.

But Jack Dash was hiding himself, folding up long spidery limbs, shrinking back into his dark corner. No one could have guessed he was an honorary prince. He looked pathetic, like a lost, frightened child.

'So what do I do now?' Maggot asked himself. He wished Gran was here. Gran would know what to do. And why didn't she tell me Jack Dash was so weird-looking, he thought accusingly.

But Maggot had no time to marvel at Gran's strange taste in boyfriends because, *Buzzzzz*, a bluebottle tickled his ear. He brushed it away.

What's that terrible stink? he thought. He'd just noticed it. '*Phew!*' It smelled like rotting meat. He looked around. And for the first time, he saw the place Jack Dash had dragged him to.

It was some kind of tiny dark room at the back of the mushroom shed. A spooky silent den, where the only light came from luminous mould and Jack's softly glowing body. There were other fungi – evil-looking ones in bright toxic colours. But it was what they surrounded, like a bodyguard, that made Maggot's eyes almost pop out of his head.

'What are they?' cried Maggot, his mouth gaping in horror.

A calm, familiar voice answered him. 'I think that's Jack's fungus – the one he brought back from his last trip. He must have managed to grow it from the spores in the spitting pot. He said it was spectacular: some kind of giant super-mushroom. He wasn't wrong, was he?'

'Gran!' said Maggot, almost fainting with relief. 'Where've you been? I was looking for you!'

But Gran was fascinated by the super-mushrooms. Maggot couldn't take his eyes off them either. These weren't silly little button mushrooms. You couldn't make fun of these. These were *serious* mushrooms.

They were shaped like monstrous eggs. Their flesh was blood-red, like raw meat.

And it wasn't smooth. It was folded and tucked, like a brain.

There was a whole tribe of them, squatting menacingly in the mushroom compost. Some were big; some were still babies. Some were already old and dying, collapsed into black slime. Bluebottle flies settled on the slime and paddled about in the mess. But the biggest super-mushroom, right in the centre, was massive, the size of a sheep.

'They're disgusting!' said Maggot. 'Yuk! They look like red brains. Did you say mushrooms were our cousins or something? That's an insult, that is! I can't believe I'm related to *them*!'

The biggest, sheep-sized one seemed to be swelling, even as Maggot watched. It looked bloated, ready to burst.

'How interesting,' Gran was saying. 'What a fascinating fungus collection. I'd no idea Jack had left all these behind. Look, here's a Destroying Angel. Here's a Satan's Boletus.'

'Interesting?' howled Maggot, who could scarcely contain himself. 'Interesting?' It made him shudder just to look at the super-

54

mushroom family. It made his skin crawl. 'How can you think they're *interesting*? What did he want to grow these for? They're gross. They're really vile! They make me sick!'

He aimed a disgusted kick at one of the baby ones. He wanted to break them up, smash them to bits, like he'd done with some slimy grey toadstools he'd once found in a field.

It was a dreadful mistake. Several things happened at once.

The baby he'd kicked oozed sticky red juice and the part where his boot had landed turned navy blue, like a bruise.

At the same time, Maggot heard shuffling behind him. He'd almost forgotten Jack Dash, huddled away in the dark. Jack came scuttling out, on all four lanky limbs, like a giant, white, top-hatted spider.

'Jack?' exclaimed Gran, in a dramatic voice. 'Jack? Is that you? I hardly recognized you. I thought you'd gone away!'

Jack Dash ignored Gran. He stood up. His burning eyes fixed on Maggot with silent hatred. As if Maggot were his deadly enemy.

'Gran!' cried Maggot, terrified. 'He's going to get me. Help! He's going to get me!'

'You leave my little flower alone!' warned Gran.

The bottle-tops jingled. Jack Dash was about to spring.

'You didn't tell me he was so weird-looking!' protested Maggot, getting ready to dodge out the way. 'You could have picked someone a bit more *normal*!'

It seemed a crazy thing to say in a moment of danger. But Maggot couldn't get it out of his head. Why hadn't Gran told him she'd chosen a freak for a boyfriend? Then he would have been prepared.

'For heaven's sake!' cried Gran. 'You don't think he was like this before, do you? *Do* credit me with some taste! I wouldn't go out with anyone looking like that. I'm not that desperate! Can't you see something terrible's happened to him? This isn't the Jack Dash I knew and loved! He's a shadow of the man I knew. Just look at him, he's a complete wreck!'

She rushed to place herself between Jack Dash and Maggot.

'Jack!' she appealed to him. 'What's got into you? It's me, Lilian. Don't you recognize me? I'm your friend!'

Maggot saw it again. He knew he did – deep down in those robot eyes. A wild, despairing look that said, 'HELP ME!', just like the message on the button mushrooms. And he even thought Jack was going to say something. He licked those flaky lips with his thick white tongue. There was a sort of noise deep in his throat, '*Hurrrrr.*' He leaned forwards, struggling to speak. '*Hurr, hurr, help murr, murr –*'

'Yes?' said Gran, trying to encourage him. 'Yes?'

KERRAK!

There was a sudden loud noise, sharp as a whip crack.

Maggot's head shot round. Then Gran's. Jack Dash's eyes glittered with a devilish light.

Something was happening to the biggest super-mushroom.

It was splitting its sides. They were cracking open like a smashed water melon.

Maggot could only stare, horrified.

KERRAK! Out of the slits shot great clouds of spores. They looked like dust. Maggot coughed and sneezed. '*Atchoo!*' They tickled his nose. He couldn't help breathing them in. The air was smoky with them.

Gran and Jack Dash were just a blur. Maggot's head whirled. He staggered about groggily in the spore haze, breathing in great, deep lungfuls.

Really strange ideas began springing up in his head. They grew, fungus-fast, until they filled his brain.

'You are one of us. You belong with us. We are *one big, happy family* now.'

Then he saw a beautiful vision.

He saw Earth, in the future. There were no cities or towns, no roads, no houses or traffic. No humans. No birdsong. No birds. Just silence, all over the planet. And super-mushrooms, crammed on to every spare centimetre of land. They'd got bigger, more brainlike, more meaty-red. Some were as big as the millennium dome! His brothers and sisters, his cousins and aunties had escaped from the mushroom farm. The giant super-mushrooms were top species. They had taken over the world!

'Yay!' shouted Maggot, punching the air.

He would do everything in his power to help them. Walk through fire. Fight off a thousand human enemies. Even lay down his own life. All to make sure his mushroom family survived and multiplied.

Nothing must stop us, thought Maggot. *Nothing.*

KERRAK! Was that somebody calling him?

'Mummy!' cried Maggot, rushing through the spore clouds to give the sheep-sized super-mushroom a great big kiss.

Suddenly he stopped dead.

What's going on? he thought, shaking his head.

His brain was clearing. Those weird thoughts and visions were flitting off, swift as bats, into the night. Soon they had vanished. In two seconds he'd forgotten completely he'd ever had them.

He stood there feeling dazed and empty-headed. And, somehow, desperately scared and alone. Like a little child who's got lost on the beach and can't find his family.

Jingle, jingle.

What's that noise? wondered Maggot, still feeling dopey.

Then came a new sound. *Clink, clink.*

I know what that is, Maggot decided groggily. That's the royal spitting pot, *ptong*. Rattling around in my baggies.

He reached a hand into his pocket. And he was just thinking, 'I haven't got it. Who's got it?' when his nose caught a strong mouldy stench. '*Phew!*' He felt breath on his neck. Cold, mushroomy breath.

AAAAARGH! Maggot's mind came crashing back to reality.

Jack Dash was right behind him! He was staring at Maggot with new savagery in his eyes. He sprang to the attack. His white fingers curled round Maggot's wrist. He seemed to have even more strength!

Maggot got his own strength from panic. 'Gerroff!' He ripped his wrist free. To think this ghoul was nearly his new grandpa! What a lucky escape.

'Gran!' he yelled. 'Run! Let's get out of here.'

KERRAK! More spores puffed out.

'I'm not going without Jack!' yelled a voice from somewhere in the grey mist.

Maggot saw a strawberry helmet. He dived towards it.

'I told you, I'm not leaving,' spluttered Gran.

'It's hopeless Gran!' said Maggot, dragging her by the arm. 'Jack Dash doesn't even know who you are! *Come on!*'

Gran stumbled after him, out of the door, into the main part of the mushroom shed. They blundered about among aisles of fungi. The twinkling mushroom-picker's lights hardly lit up the dark at all.

Maggot tripped, shot out a hand to save himself. '*Ugggh!*' and ended up with a fistful of squelchy Stinkhorn.

There was that jingly noise again! He turned round. And gasped out loud with shock. It wasn't only Gran who was following him. At the far end of the aisle he could see a glowing shape in the gloom. It was moving their way with deadly speed. Jack Dash, in his top hat, with his bottle-top necklace jangling, was hot on their trail.

'Hurry up, Gran! Look, here's the way out!'

But Jack was loping behind them, his tail-coat flapping!

Maggot yanked the door open for Gran. She ran through. He was about to race after her when a white claw closed on his ankle, with a grip like iron.

Maggot went berserk. He kicked out in a frenzy, dived for the sunshine. The claw melted away. He was free!

He rolled over and over in the dusty yard, staggered to his knees, coughing, but ready to run again. He glanced back at the shed and saw instantly that he didn't have to run any more. Jack Dash wasn't following them. He was in the doorway. But he was shrinking back from the strong sunlight, shielding his eyes as if they hurt him.

He doesn't like sunlight, thought Maggot. He wants to stay in the dark.

Jack Dash's eyes blazed fiercely at Maggot. He still wanted to get him. He took a step outside. Then suddenly he crumpled to the ground, squirming like a white worm.

Maggot stared, horrified. While Jack Dash thrashed about, powdery spores puffed out through the mouldy wedding suit. They came from his neck, from his hands, from his clammy white skin. Just as if he were a fungus too.

He's not a man! Maggot twigged, with a sudden flash of understanding. He's changing into a mushroom! Jack Dash is half man, half mushroom!

For a few seconds, Jack Dash stayed in a pathetic heap, curled up and helpless, hiding his eyes from the light. Then a cloud slid over the sun. And he began to crawl, very slowly and painfully. Sneaking back into the shed, like a wounded animal. He clutched blindly at the doorpost, dragged himself back into the dark. The shed door slammed shut behind him. He was gone.

On shaky legs, Maggot walked to where the mushroom-man had fallen. And where he had lifted himself up to crawl, Maggot saw Jack Dash had left a spore print – a perfect impression of his hand.

Maggot knelt down to look at it. It brought a lump to his throat. He was thinking about the wild, bold adventurer Jack Dash had once been.

Then suddenly he remembered Gran. What must she be thinking about all this? Bet she thinks she had a lucky escape too, he decided. After all, she nearly married a mushroom. Or someone who's ninety-nine per cent mushroom anyway.

Jack Dash wasn't one hundred per cent mushroom yet, Maggot reminded himself. What about those pleading looks? Didn't they show that there was still a human being in there somewhere, desperately trying to get out?

What about the messages on those mushrooms? Help me? Save me? What about that tragic little face? Maggot was sure now that Jack Dash had carved them, as a last cry for help, before the creeping mushroom disease took over his entire body.

He looked round for Gran. They had a lot of talking to do. She must be in state of shock, thought Maggot. It's not every day you find out that your fiancé is almost a fungus.

He'd already got some words of comfort ready. 'At least Jack Dash didn't run out on you, Gran,' he was going to say. 'He was here at the mushroom farm all the time.'

He still couldn't see her. Where had she got to? He was just anxiously shouting, 'Gran!' when he felt breath on his neck. Not warm human breath. But cold, clammy, mushroomy breath.

Oh no, thought Maggot. Oh no. Not Gran. Please don't let it be Gran.

Chapter Seven

Gran was right there behind him. She had sneaked up on him, silently, fungus-fast.

And Maggot saw straightaway that the unthinkable was happening. Gran was changing into a mushroom too. It was her eyes mainly. They were already lighter. Soon they would be as pale as pearls. She would develop a mushroom's strength and begin to glow in the dark. Her flesh would turn rubbery and start puffing out spores.

It was a nightmare. Suddenly Maggot's brain couldn't cope any more. It was going berserk, like a crashing computer, throwing up all kinds of wild, crazy images. He saw Gran, sprouting from underground, pushing up paving stones with her strawberry helmet. And leaving spore prints on everything she touched.

This isn't happening to me! It's not real! It's all a bad dream! thought Maggot wildly, clutching his poor spinning head in his hands.

Then he saw Gran take a few stiff, robot steps. She was heading for the shed – the one where Jack Dash lurked in the dark, protecting the sinister super-mushrooms. Soon she would be inside the door.

And Maggot couldn't pretend it wasn't real any longer.

With a superhuman effort, he got his brain back under control. He sprang into action.

Maggot flung himself at Gran, barring her way to the mushroom shed.

'Gran!' he yelled. 'Don't go in there!' He had the sickening feeling that once she went in, he'd lost her.

But Gran took no notice. Her zombie eyes looked right through him. They were fixed on that mushroom shed door.

'Gran!' screamed Maggot frantically. 'Come back!'

He tried again to stop her. But like Jack Dash, she was fearfully strong. She batted him out the way, as if he were a gnat.

'You hit me!' said Maggot, shocked and surprised. 'No offence, Gran, but that really hurt!'

He rugby-tackled her legs, clung like a sucker fish to her ankles. But she dragged him along in the dust behind her, then easily kicked him off and left him sprawling in the dust.

'Gran!'

It was too late. Someone opened the shed door for her. Maggot glimpsed the gleam of white eyes inside. Then Gran slipped through and vanished into the gloom.

'Oh, Gran! Now they've got you too!'

Maggot beat his fists on the ground, in rage and despair at his own helplessness. What was he going to tell his mum? How could he ring her up from Gran's house and say, 'Er, Mum, now don't start shouting, cos it's not my fault, honest, so promise me you won't get mad. But – but Gran's turning into a mushroom – '?

It made him shudder, like a double dose of Gran's green tea, just imagining Mum's reaction.

He couldn't face it. He was feeling far too fragile at the moment.

He paced up and down outside the mushroom shed, even though he knew, in his heart, Gran wasn't coming out.

He thought, I'll go in there and get her!

But he knew that would be stupid.

Jack Dash would be on guard, looking out for intruders. He'd attack any strangers. Anyone he thought threatened his precious super-mushrooms. As soon as he showed his face, Maggot knew he'd be pounced on and gripped by those rubbery octopus arms.

And what about Gran? Whose side would she be on? Maggot didn't even want to think about that.

He hung around for ages, just watching the sheds, waiting for something to happen. But nothing did. Nothing at all. The place seemed dead. Nothing moved in the hot sunshine. The shed where the super-mushrooms lived looked deserted. Only Maggot knew of the horrors waiting inside.

As he watched, his mind was a whirlpool of questions. How did Gran catch the creeping mushroom disease and not me? How did Jack Dash catch it? Why are they both turning into mushrooms and I'm not?

His mind had mercifully blocked out those mad mushroom moments when he too, just for a few seconds, had been a slave.

At least I hope I'm not! thought Maggot. Anxiously he poked out his tongue out and inspected it, cross-eyed. It didn't seem to have gone white. His skin didn't feel rubbery. He blew into his cupped hand and had a careful sniff.

What a pong! thought Maggot, reeling back in disgust from his own breath. But it wasn't a mouldy mushroom stink. It was the even fouler stench of Gran's toxic tea.

Phew, that's a relief, thought Maggot.

But another question sprang up to torment him. What'll happen to Gran and

Jack Dash when they become completely one hundred per cent fungus?

Maybe, he thought, they'll die like other fungi do. Dissolve into big pools of sticky black slime. Or shrivel to dry, feather-light husks and blow away in the wind. Puff balls did that. He'd seen them.

'This is awful!' cried Maggot in growing anguish. He was at his wit's end. He didn't know what to do next. His brain felt like it was going to explode.

'You can't deal with this on your own,' he told himself. 'You need some back-up.'

At last, he'd made some kind of decision. He raced out of the mushroom farm, clashing the gate shut behind him.

He left Gran's ancient bone-shaker bike where it was and went whizzing off on her high-speed bicycle. He was going so fast the pea fields were just a green blur.

He threw the bike down in Gran's garden. He didn't have a door key – that was in Gran's bumbag. But that didn't hold him up. He just stood on the water butt and wriggled through the open conservatory window.

He skidded through into the hall where the phone was. He lifted the receiver. His finger prepared to stab a number.

Maggot meant to phone his big brother. That would be the best thing to do. Nigel was sixteen. He was a serious-minded person. He was taking important exams at school. He would know how to sort this mess out.

But somehow Maggot's finger disobeyed him. At the very last moment it changed direction and punched in Spud's number.

My loyal mate Spud won't let me down! thought Maggot. He and Spud had been friends for almost their whole lives. They had been to toddler group together, then playschool. And now they were both in Miss Miller's class at Silver Street School.

The phone rang for a long time. 'Come on, come on, come on!' fretted Maggot.

At last, someone picked it up.

'Yep?' said a groggy voice.

'Spud!' Maggot yelled down the phone. 'Are you listening, Spud? You've got to come to Gran's *now*! I need your help. You wouldn't *believe* what's been going on down here! For a start –'

'Do you know what time it is?' howled an outraged voice at the other end of the line.

'No.' Maggot had no idea. Time didn't seem to matter in the mushroom sheds. Ages could've passed. Days, years. He checked his watch and was amazed to find that it was only half past nine.

'You've woken me up!' bellowed Spud down the phone. 'I'm not even awake yet! And when I'm awake I'm going to watch the cartoons on telly. So don't ring me again. Not until this afternoon.'

Maggot's eardrum rattled as the phone was slammed down.

'Huh!' said Maggot in an aggrieved voice. 'Huh!'

He'd forgotten Spud wasn't an early riser. That, in the holidays, he rarely crawled out of his duvet before midday.

Only one thing for it, thought Maggot. He'd have to call his big brother. *He* was always up bright and early.

'I should have done that before,' Maggot

told himself. 'That Spud is useless. He wouldn't have been any help at all! In fact, he'd have got in my way.'

Brrr, brrr; brrr, brrr.

'Hello?'

Maggot's stomach clenched up, tight as a fist. Oh no, it's Mum! he thought in a panic.

He tried to make his voice as normal as possible. But it still sounded strange and shrill. 'Er, Mum, is Nigel there?' he said, in his new warbly voice.

'He's practising his trumpet,' said Mum. Maggot could hear a loud mooing noise, like a sick cow, in the background. 'Why, what do you want him for?'

'Oh, nothing,' said Maggot hopelessly. 'It doesn't matter.'

Instantly, Mum was suspicious. 'Is Gran all right?' she interrogated him. 'There's nothing wrong, is there? Are you coming back home today?'

Maggot felt suddenly really weary. All these questions, he couldn't handle them. For a nanosecond he was tempted to tell Mum the whole story. But he knew he couldn't handle that either. Mum didn't even know Gran had been secretly planning to marry Jack Dash. That would send her into fits. And that was just the beginning!

Maggot groaned and shook his head.

'Are you all right?' said Mum, sharp as a tack.

'Yep, yep, yep,' burbled Maggot, cranking his voice up so it sounded idiotically chirpy and cheery. 'I'm fine and Gran is fine, we're all fine and I'm being really good and I'm brushing my teeth and I'm not picking my athlete's foot and I'm staying here tonight so I'll ring you tomorrow and I'm going now and –'

'Wait!' Mum's stern command rang in his ears.

'Er, what?' said Maggot, his heart fluttering.

'What did you want Nigel for?' demanded Mum.

'Er, er –' Maggot's brain raced round like a squirrel in a cage. 'I wanted to tell him this good joke I heard.'

'What joke?' asked Mum.

Why does she keep asking me *questions*? thought Maggot, nearly demented. If she didn't ask me so many *questions*. I wouldn't have to tell all these lies!

'What joke?' repeated Mum. 'I like a good joke.'

'Er, Er – ' Maggot heard that horrible mooing noise in the background. Suddenly, *ping*, a light came on in his brain. He almost fainted with relief. 'This joke,' he gabbled into the phone. 'Right? Are you listening? Here it comes. Two cows in a field. Right? And one says to the other: "Mooo!" And the other one says, "Hey! I was going to say that!"'

There was complete silence at the other end of the line.

Then, 'Yes?' said Mum, in a baffled voice.

'That's it,' said Maggot. 'Don't you get it? Two cows in a field and one says – '

'Yes, yes, I heard you the first time,' said Mum. 'I'll tell Nigel, when he's finished playing his trumpet. Maybe he'll explain it to me.'

'No offence, Mum, *arf, arf,*' coughed Maggot. 'But you've got absolutely no sense of humour. Anyway, bye, Mum! Bye, bye. Yes, bye. Phone you tomorrow! No, Gran can't talk to you now. No, bye!' Maggot slapped the phone down before Mum could think up any more awkward questions.

'*Phew!*' He slumped against the wall. I'm sweating now! he thought. That was a very close call. Give Mum half a chance and she locked on to lies like a lie-seeking missile.

Maggot let himself slowly slide down the wall until he was sitting on the carpet. He gave a deep, lonely sigh.

It had suddenly struck him what an awful situation he was in.

'I'm all on my own now!' he complained out loud in a voice full of angry self-pity. 'Jack Dash is a mushroom! Gran is a mushroom! Spud is watching cartoons! What am I supposed to do on my own, against those super-fungus things? I'm only a kid.'

If only Jack Dash was on his side, he thought. Jack Dash, as he had been in the old days, before he became a mushroom. When he had a mind of his own. When he was a mad, reckless, daredevil botanist. A lion-wrestling, pee-drinking hero who was red-hot at spitting.

We would have sorted things out, no problem, *pting*, thought Maggot wistfully. Me and Jack Dash. If only he was like he was before. If only he was on my side.

But Maggot knew that was too many 'if onlys'. He knew he was wishing for the moon.

He wandered miserably into the kitchen. He hardly knew what he was doing. He took some dry cornflakes out of the box and munched them. Without thinking, he washed them down with a swig from a mug on the table.

Oh no, he thought, his face creased like a goblin's. What did I do that for? That's Gran's terrible tea!

He had to get a grip on himself. It wasn't doing Gran and Jack Dash any good at all, going to pieces like this.

Maggot took a deep breath. Time to give himself a quick pep talk. 'Jack Dash wouldn't have moped around being all useless!' he told himself sternly. 'He was a man of action! He'd have made a plan!'

Maggot thought of that shed on the silent farm in the middle of pea fields. Icy-cold shivers chased down his spine. What was going on in there? He couldn't imagine how mushrooms spent their day. Did Gran and Jack Dash try to communicate, with those chalky white lips? Or did they move round slyly, fungus-quiet in the dark, guarding the super mushrooms, giving them fresh compost whenever they needed it?

He felt totally out of his depth. I wish I was an expert on fungi like Jack Dash, he thought.

Then, to his amazement, a plan appeared in his brain. It just plopped in there, like a fat frog plopping into a pond.

'I know!' cried Maggot. 'I'll *make* myself into an expert! I'll go back to Jack's caravan. Have a look at some of his books. And then I'll know what to do next. No problem!'

He went racing out of Gran's house. He left the back door on the latch so he could get back in, hopped on Gran's bike and pedalled madly away through the pea fields. In the distance, red monster machines trundled across the skyline, harvesting peas. Apart from Maggot, they were the only things moving in the big empty landscape. But Maggot didn't even notice them.

At the mushroom farm he leapt off the bike, dashed into Jack's caravan and quickly scanned the shelves of books.

This one! he thought.

It was called, *Fascinating Facts about Fungi*. He yanked it off the shelf, dumped it on the tiny caravan table, and began frantically flicking through it.

He had no idea what he was looking for. And, besides, he was so twitchy that nothing he read made any sense. The print was just a blur.

'Useless boring book!' cried Maggot impatiently, hurling it on to the floor. 'It's rubbish that book is!'

Becoming a mushroom expert wasn't as easy as he thought.

I should be rescuing Gran and Jack Dash,

he fretted. Not wasting time reading stupid old books!

He pulled out another one. It was just the same. His jittery brain just wouldn't take it in.

Stupid boring book!

His hopes, that had just been sky-high, went crashing down to earth like the poor World War Two pilot's plane.

He almost hurled the book away like the first one.

Then something caught his eye.

'What's this all about?' thought Maggot, suddenly excited.

He pulled the book under his nose to study a photograph.

It was a black and white picture of a shrivelled fly, with spores puffing out of its body.

Feverishly, he read what it said under the photo, following the lines of tiny print with a shaky finger.

'This unfortunate fly,' the book told him, *'has been infected by a fungus. It breathed in the spores through its spiracles, the breathing holes in its body. Once*

inside the fly, the fungus begins its deadly progress. It travels through the fly's body. It takes over. The fly's body becomes fungus-like. Spores even infect the fly's brain, making it behave in strange and unusual ways. In the last stages, spores begin to puff out of its body. Then, slowly, the fly becomes completely fungified.'

'*Arghhh!*' cried Maggot, dropping the book as if it could infect him with fungus spores. He didn't need to read any more. He slumped against the table, weak with shock.

'It was the spores!' he gasped. 'The giant super-mushroom spores infected Jack Dash and then Gran. They breathed them in. And the spores started infecting their body and brain. Made them behave in strange and unusual ways. Just like the book says.'

He picked the book up again. He didn't want to, but he had to remind himself of the last bit. '*In the last stages, spores begin to puff out of its body,*' he read in a quaking voice. '*Then, slowly, the fly becomes completely fungified.*'

He put his head in his hands. The terrible consequences of what he'd just read were springing up in his mind like monsters.

'Jack Dash is in the last stages,' he whispered. 'And soon he'll become completely fungified. And then the same thing'll happen to Gran! I wonder how long it takes to spread?' He remembered Gran saying, 'Some fungi are really fast movers.'

Maybe it only takes days – or hours! Maggot thought, horrified.

With a trembling hand, he turned over the page in the book. It didn't say anything about how long it took. But there was a dreadful photo of a totally fungified fly. It was just a withered, empty shell. *Puff*, you could blow it off your palm like a dry leaf. Maggot forced himself to look at it.

'So that's how they'll end up,' he told himself, appalled.

A ghoulish picture came into his head of his gran, totally fungified. She was a dry husk, a shrivelled, brown, mummified thing. He only knew it was her because she was still wearing her strawberry helmet and her bright orange shorts with 'N.E. LINCS ROAD RACING CLUB' in gold letters on the side.

'It's too horrible, I can't stand it!' Maggot cried out, trying to block the nightmare picture out of his mind. 'I've got to do something! I've got to save them!'

Chapter Eight

Maggot sat for a long time in Jack Dash's caravan. Through the windows he could see the mushroom sheds, sinister and still in the dazzling sunlight.

He didn't expect anyone to come out. There were no clouds today. The sky over the pea fields was perfect blue. If Gran and Jack Dash were going to sneak out, it wouldn't be for ages yet, not until after sunset, when the light didn't hurt their eyes. He couldn't wait that long. Gran had to be rescued ASAP. With every hour that passed, she would become less like Gran and more and more like a mushroom.

'So what's your plan then?' Maggot asked himself sternly. He didn't expect a reply. He had no plan. Everything was tangled up in his head, like washing in a spin dryer.

The same questions, though, kept whirling round to the front of his brain. Why them? Why them and not me? I breathed in the spores. Why isn't my body going all white and rubbery, right this minute? Why isn't *my* brain infected?

He couldn't work it out. It was too big a problem. It just made his head ache.

Absent-mindedly, he pulled at his lower lip. Then picked at his teeth. It didn't help him to think. But it did leave him with a speck of bright green gunge on the tip of his finger.

What's that? wondered Maggot, inspecting it closely. Is that spinach? I haven't eaten spinach for three weeks, not since the last time at Gran's. Surely I must've brushed my teeth since then!

Then he realized what it was. Phew, that's all right, he thought. It's only a bit of Gran's horrible green tea.

Ping! His brain lit up like an airport runway.

Wow, marvelled Maggot, stunned by his own brilliance.

'It was the tea!' he whispered to himself. 'The tea stopped me getting infected – it made me immune.'

His brain was racing ahead now, tripping over itself. The more he thought about it, the more it made sense.

'Gran said it would kill any infection stone-dead,' he told himself excitedly. 'She said it was a natural antibiotic, *strong* medicine. She said it could kill my foot fungus and that's *really* disgusting. So I bet it could easily kill those super-mushroom spores.'

Maggot thought of Gran's green tea surging around his body, zapping spores wherever it found them, like evil aliens in a computer game. The thought made him feel powerful and strong. For the first time in ages, he didn't feel totally helpless. He had an ally against the all-powerful super-mushrooms! He felt a strange feeling fizzing away inside him. It was hope.

For the second time that morning, Maggot went racing back through the pea fields.

He burst into Gran's kitchen and began feverishly searching through the cupboards. He yanked open door after door.

'Where is it? Where is it?' he chanted anxiously to himself.

The cupboards were crammed with stuff. Old, yellowing newspapers, bits of string, empty lemonade bottles. Gran was a great hoarder; she never threw anything away.

At last, he found something. In a wall cupboard there was an old cloth bag with a drawstring at the top. He opened it. A musty, spicy smell came out.

Is this it? wondered Maggot.

It wasn't green. It was full of brown, dried-up things – bits of bark, flowers, moss, strange seed pods. Something that looked horribly like a tiny, withered frog.

He turned on the kettle, waited for it to warm up. He shook some of the dried stuff into a jug, sloshed on some hot water.

Bingo! It instantly turned a bright, glowing green.

That's it! thought Maggot triumphantly.

Gran always strained the tea before she

dosed him with it. No wonder she does that, thought Maggot. She doesn't want me to see what's in it!

But he had no time for things like that. He just made up a few litres, quick as he could, and filled some of Gran's empty bottles.

He shook one. The gunk on the bottom swirled around like a green snow storm. Was that a plump, re-hydrated caterpillar he saw bobbing about?

But this was a matter of life and death. Maggot had no time to be squeamish. He closed his eyes, tilted his head back, and took a few glugs. He had to make sure he was still immune. He kept his teeth gritted though, to strain out the largest of those suspicious floating objects.

'Backpack, backpack, backpack!' chanted Maggot, yanking open some more doors. He wished he'd come on Gran's ancient bike, then he could have loaded the bottles in the basket.

'This'll do!'

He grabbed Gran's luminous yellow road-racing backpack. It still had a big number ten on it from her last race. He stashed the bottles of tea inside.

With the bottles clinking on his back, he leapt on to Gran's bike. They were so heavy he wobbled at first, almost fell off. Then he got going, pedalling like the wind towards the mushroom farm.

The same picture in his head kept tormenting him. It just wouldn't go away. He saw Gran and Jack Dash, completely fungified. Like the fly in the photo, they were just shrivelled husks, crispy as cornflakes, light as feathers, blowing away over the pea fields.

This tea had better work, thought Maggot desperately. It had better cure them. It's just *got* to!

Chapter Nine

The mushroom farm seemed as lifeless as ever. But this time Maggot didn't spy on it from the pea fields. Or watch it through the windows of Jack Dash's caravan. He knew exactly what he had to do. Gran and Jack Dash weren't going to come out in the sunshine. They might not come out at all. So he had to go in and get them. He had no choice.

He walked slowly through the gate. The shed where the giant super-mushrooms lived seemed to be waiting for him – silent, menacing.

He squatted on the ground, unslung his backpack and pulled out a bottle of Gran's green tea.

If you ignored the thick layer of sludge, it looked a bit like limeade. The bright green kind Mum got at the supermarket. Suddenly doubts flooded Maggot's mind.

'What if it doesn't work?' he whispered to himself.

It didn't *look* as if it could kill super-mushroom spores. He had no evidence at all that it could stop Gran being fungified.

Yet it was his only hope.

'You'll never find out if it works if you stay here!' he told himself sternly.

He swallowed hard, once, twice. Then gripped the bottle as if it was a powerful weapon. Before he could argue himself out of it, he strode across the yard and through the shed door, into the blackness.

His nose caught the strong whiff of mouldy graveyards. The tiny mushroom-picker's lights were still twinkling. By their feeble glimmer, he could see a thousand freaky fungi: blue and warty, black and greasy, soft and see-through like raspberry jelly.

Where were Gran and Jack Dash?

Probably in that other room, protecting the giant super-mushrooms.

He crept along a dark aisle. Fungi crowded around him on both sides.

Something licked his face. *'Ugghh!'* He leapt aside. But it was only a grey slimy fungus, shaped like a tongue.

He heard shuffling in the shadows. He spun round, his heart thumping . . .

. . . And saw a flash of orange lycra – a wobbling strawberry helmet. 'Gran, thank goodness it's only you!' he gasped, weak with relief. 'I thought it was Jack Dash!'

Gran said nothing. She was mushroom-quiet.

She fixed him with sly, pale eyes that glowed in the gloom.

Maggot gabbled on. 'Gran! I've brought some stuff to make you better. And guess what? It's your tea!' He shook the bottle at her. The green snowstorm swirled. 'Remember you said it'd kill any infection stone-dead? Well, I think it'll kill super-mushroom spores. Go on, Gran, drink it!' He started to unscrew the top.

Gran crouched down on her wiry bicycling legs, like a cat ready to spring.

'Gran!' said Maggot, seriously alarmed. 'I've come to rescue you!'

But Gran didn't want to be rescued. She was with her fungus family, where she belonged. And Maggot was the stranger, the intruder.

'It's me – your little flower!' he cried desperately, jabbing away at his chest.

But there was no recognition in Gran's eyes. They glittered at him menacingly, from under the cycling helmet.

Oh no! thought Maggot. She thinks she's a mushroom! Those spores are already infecting her brain. It's well scrambled!

She was going to attack him.

Maggot still couldn't believe it. His own gran!

He backed off. He held out a hand, palm-up, trying to calm her down.

'I've just come to get you out of here,' he explained frantically. 'I'm not going to hurt your giant super-mushrooms, honest I'm not. I think they're lovely, I really do. I'm

94

their biggest fan.' He almost added, 'I've come to get their autographs,' as if they were a chart-topping pop group, but even his panicky brain realized, that's ridiculous!

Gran lunged at him. Maggot dodged out her way.

'Gran, it's me!' he cried, yet again, even though he knew it was hopeless.

Gran's eyes blazed even more fiercely.

She was closing in! She grabbed his wrist.

'Ow!' Maggot had forgotten about her terrible mushroom strength.

She's like Superwoman! thought Maggot, nearly out of his mind with fear.

He wrenched his wrist away, but Gran moved in, dancing about like a boxer. Her arm shot out. This time, Maggot dropped to the floor, rolled up like an armadillo. Gran tripped over him. Her helmet must have come loose; it rolled off into the dark.

Did she crack her head on a mushroom bed? Maggot wasn't sure. It all happened so fast.

She struggled to her knees, but she looked dizzy. She was shaking her head.

Maggot saw his chance. But he had to be quick.

'Drink this, Gran!'

He crouched beside her, took the top off the bottle. He tipped it up and glugged the tea straight down Gran's throat.

She choked and coughed. Bright green tea spilled down her T-shirt. But she swallowed an awful lot.

Maggot shook the bottle. It was almost empty.

'Gran, how do you feel?' Maggot begged her. 'Do you know who I am?'

Gran's face turned, very slowly, towards him. Maggot gasped. Her eyes were still alien eyes! They still blazed at him as if he was the enemy.

'It's not working,' Maggot's brain gibbered at him. 'Run! It's not working!'

But he couldn't run. He couldn't *abandon* Gran. Leave her to be a slave to the giant super-mushrooms. To breathe in more and more spores. Until she got totally fungified. And then, and then – but Maggot didn't have time to picture that last nightmare stage, where Gran blew away like a dried-up puffball. Because his ears had just picked up a very faint sound.

Jingle, jingle; clink, clink.

'Jack Dash!' Maggot shrieked out loud.

He would have to run now. Run for his life.

He was already on his feet for a flying start when a shaky voice demanded, 'Where's my helmet? That cost me a fortune, that did.'

'Gran!' Maggot peered closely at her. 'Do you know who I am?'

'Course I do! Not know my own grandson! I'm not senile yet, you know!'

A great grin broke out over Maggot's face. 'You know me! You know me!'

But he didn't have time to celebrate. He could see a white blurry glow in the shadows. It was Jack Dash, prowling down the aisle, on long rubbery legs. Even from this distance, Maggot could see spores puffing out through his top hat. They glittered in the mushroom-picker's lights.

'Come on, Gran!' He hauled her to her feet and scooped up her helmet. 'I've got no more medicine for Jack in here. It's outside!'

Even as he said this, it flashed through his mind, 'He's too far gone for medicine. He's one hundred per cent mushroom.'

Gran and Maggot raced for the shed door. Gran was fitter, she reached it first. Maggot stumbled. 'He's got me!'

But it was only some electric wires, tangling his feet. He ripped himself free. As he did, there was a shower of sparks somewhere and all the little mushroom-picker's lights went out.

In the pitch blackness, there was a tiny wisp of smoke. Then a smell of burning.

But Maggot didn't notice. He was too busy trying to escape. He crashed out of the shed, into the yard. Ran until he bounced off the wire fence. It was only then that he turned to look back.

'We made it!' he cheered. 'We made it!'

He began pulling more bottles of green tea out his backpack.

'Here, Gran,' he said. 'Better drink some more of this. Drink as much as you can. There's plenty for Jack.'

'He won't come out into the light,' Gran said. 'They hate the daylight. They like to stay in the dark.'

For the first time, Maggot really looked at Gran. 'You all right, Gran?' he asked her anxiously, as she gulped down another dose of green tea.

'Yes, my flower,' said Gran shakily. 'Thanks to you. You're a right little hero, you are.'

Maggot grinned modestly. But his chest swelled with pride.

Gran looked rather droopy and pale. She seemed worn out, as if she'd had a really bad day. But she was recovering fast. Sunlight didn't upset her. And her eyes were Gran's eyes. They weren't mushroom eyes any more.

Just to make sure, Maggot urged her, 'Have another drink!'

'This stuff's really foul!' complained Gran, wiping her mouth with the back of her hand.

'That shows it's doing you good,' said Maggot. 'You have a rest, Gran. You stay here.'

He looked back towards the mushroom shed. Jack Dash wasn't going to come out. That meant he, Maggot, was going to have to go back in.

He thought of that spooky back room, lit by the ghostly glow of mould and mildew, where giant super-mushrooms crouched in compost, swelling until they went '*KERRAK!*'

He shuddered, took several deep breaths, and armed himself with a couple of bottles of Gran's green tea.

Then Gran yelled, 'The mushroom shed's on fire! And Jack's still inside!'

'What? I can't see anything.'

'There!' said Gran, pointing. 'There. Up on the roof!'

Tiny flames, like fiery squirrels, were racing along the roof. Suddenly the shed began leaking smoke. It was curling out between the planks. Then, *whoosh*, one of the shuttered windows burst open. Maggot could see a strange crimson glow, deep inside.

The shed door crashed open. Jack Dash came staggering out, coughing and choking. Thick black smoke rolled out after him.

Jack tried to run. Then collapsed in the yard, protecting his eyes with his hands.

'Quick! yelled Gran. 'Get that tea down his neck!'

Maggot knelt by Jack Dash. He noticed how smooth and unwrinkled Jack's skin was. Just like a white button mushroom. 'Here, drink this!' he said, trickling some green tea down Jack's throat. The heat from the fire was scorching his back. It was raging fiercely now. The whole shed was ablaze.

But the tea wasn't working. Jack was thrashing about. He was on the move, trying to crawl back into the mushroom shed.

'Stop him!' yelled Gran. 'He's trying to save the fungus!'

Maggot threw himself at Jack Dash. But Jack's old lion-wrestling skills weren't quite dead yet. He got Maggot in a head-lock.

'Gerroff!' cried Maggot. 'You freaky fungus! Let me go!'

But Jack wasn't hurting him. He was being deliberately gentle. He put his flaky white lips close to Maggot's ear. His voice was a croak. 'Too late for me!' the voice said. 'Too late!' Then it went quiet.

Maggot couldn't believe he'd heard it. Astonished, he looked deep into Jack Dash's eyes. But his human brain had finally shut down. There was nothing there. Nothing at all.

They've got him, thought Maggot, shaking his head in despair. He's mushroom through and through.

Jack shot sideways like a crab. Maggot did a flying tackle. He grabbed the tails of Jack's wedding coat. The mildewed material just came away in his hands.

'I can't stop him,' gasped Maggot, rolling out the way of Jack's kicking feet. 'He's too strong! He's getting away!'

Gran was rested now. She rushed over to help. But there was nothing anyone could do.

'Jack!' she shouted. But Jack had already slipped through the door, into the blazing shed.

All that was left was a trail of spore prints from his scuttling hands and feet.

Maggot was sure Gran was going to rush after Jack. He got ready to hold her back.

But suddenly, *WHUMP!* There was a blinding flash. Gran and Maggot staggered back, shielding their eyes.

'Get down!' shouted Gran.

Maggot flung himself face-down in the dust.

One end of the shed appeared to explode. Then the whole shed seemed to lift off the ground. The mushroom spores had acted like gunpowder. A great jet of pink flame shot into the sky. It turned to a roaring blue. Burning spores whizzed and crackled and popped like fireworks.

Jack Dash stood no chance at all in that inferno.

Did Maggot hear screams of rage and defiance from the frying super-mushrooms? At the time he thought he did. But later he told himself, 'No, you probably imagined it.'

Maggot covered his head and pressed his face in the dirt as bits of charred wood and ashes rained down.

Suddenly the roaring stopped. All Maggot

could hear was silence. Cautiously, he lifted his head. He couldn't believe what he saw. The mushroom shed seemed to have evaporated. In its place was a black smoking hole in the ground.

Stunned with shock, Maggot and Gran gazed at the place where the shed had been. They stood there for ages, just staring.

Maggot's head was as empty as a swimming pool after closing time. But Gran must have been doing some fast thinking because, when she finally spoke, she said, 'It was all for the best.'

'What?' said Maggot, coming out of his trance. 'What did you say, Gran?'

A few cinders were still drifting down.

'Well,' said Gran, 'that *thing* in the mushroom shed – that wasn't my Jack. Not Jack like he used to be. That's the Jack I'm going to remember,' said Gran, with pride in her voice, 'a mad adventuring botanist, an honorary prince, a lion-wrestling hero!'

'And a pee-drinker and seagull snacker,' Maggot reminded her.

'Yes! He was all of those things!' agreed

Gran fondly. 'He wasn't that blank-eyed zombie you saw in the mushroom shed. I wish you'd known the real Jack Dash,' said Gran with a tear in her eye. 'The Jack that he used to be.'

Suddenly Maggot recalled Jack Dash's last whispering words before he rushed back into the fire. 'Too late. It's too late for me.'

And Maggot realized that he *had* known the real Jack Dash. As Jack battled against fungification, before his brain was totally taken over, Maggot had had a brief glimpse of the Jack that used to be.

I think Jack Dash knew he was doomed, Maggot was thinking. His own lips were trembling too. He was struggling not to cry. I think he knew there was no hope. So he went back into the fire. He was a hero to the end! He never stopped being a hero!

And, as if she was reading his mind, Gran asked him sharply. 'When Jack had you in that headlock, I thought I saw him whisper something in your ear. But I'm being silly, aren't I? I must have made a mistake.'

Maggot hesitated. 'Er.' His mind was

tugged this way, that way. Then he told the most whopping lie he'd ever told in his life. He told it because he thought it would spare Gran more pain. He didn't want her to know how much Jack had suffered.

'You made a mistake, Gran,' he said. 'How could Jack Dash say anything? He wasn't Jack any more. His body and brain had been totally taken over. He was in the last stages of fungification. Just like the fly in the photo.'

'Eh?' said Gran. 'What you talking about. What fly? What photo?' Her sinewy cycling legs went suddenly shaky. She sat down on the ground. 'I don't understand anything, my flower. I think I've gone totally doolally. What happened to poor Jack? What's been happening to me?'

'Well,' began Maggot, taking a deep breath, 'you're not going to believe this, Gran, but – '

Chapter Ten

'And that's just about it, Gran,' said Maggot. He'd finished his explanation. He'd been pacing up and down, up and down. He always thought better on the move.

He hadn't lied this time, like he had about Jack's last words. But he had glossed over some details. He hadn't told Gran *exactly* what happened, at the very end, to fungified people. After all she'd been through, he thought it would be just too upsetting.

'But there are still lots of things I don't understand,' Maggot finished up, with a puzzled frown. 'When Jack Dash went to the jungle, to collect the giant super-mushrooms, why wasn't he infected out there? I bet he breathed in loads of fungus spores.'

'Because he drank the green tea of course,' said Gran. 'Like everyone else in the village. He had to – just to be polite. But he stopped as soon as he came home. He said it made him feel sick.'

'I know what he means,' said Maggot.

'Actually,' said Gran, tipping a bottle up and taking a swig. 'I could get to like it. It's miraculous stuff. Look it's cured all my symptoms.' Gran stuck her tongue out. It was healthy pink again. 'Although I quite liked being wrinkle-free and immensely strong,' added Gran, almost wistfully. 'Being a mushroom had its good points.'

'You don't mean that, Gran!' said Maggot, appalled.

'You know me,' said Gran. 'Just trying to look on the bright side.'

Then, to his alarm, Maggot saw Gran's face crumple. For a moment, she looked really sad. 'It wouldn't have worked out, my flower, would it?' she asked him.

'What, you and Jack Dash? No, Gran,'

said Maggot, trying his best to be tactful. 'He was too far gone. It was too late. Even the green tea couldn't help him.'

'Poor Jack,' sighed Gran. 'I don't know what I'm going to tell them at Moss Bros.'

'But there's one *really* good thing,' said Maggot, desperate to cheer Gran up. 'At least those giant super-mushrooms are dead.' He looked at the burnt-out crater where the shed had been. 'And all the spores are sizzled. At least they can't infect anyone else.'

He was still pacing about. A wind had come up. It brought a fresh green-pea smell, from the pea fields, to mix with the smell of fried mushrooms.

Clink.

Maggot froze. He knew that sound. He hardly dared hope! He looked down.

'It's the royal spitting pot!' he said, in an awed voice. 'It must have fallen out of Jack's pocket!'

Maggot pounced on the pot, cradling it lovingly in his hands. He wiped off the black smuts from the mysterious signs and symbols.

Then turned the pot round so it glinted silver in the light.

'Here you are,' he said, handing the pot over to Gran.

'No, you have it,' she told Maggot. 'You're the hero of the hour. If it hadn't been for you, I'd still be in that shed thinking I was a mushroom!'

'Can I really have it?' said Maggot, thrilled to bits. He just had to try something. He took the lid off the pot. Then placed it carefully on the ground. He stepped back a few paces, puckered up his lips. '*Pting!*' And another one. '*Ptong!*'

'Brilliant shot!' Gran applauded. 'Brilliant! Jack Dash couldn't have done better.'

Maggot was embarrassed at all this praise. He wasn't used to it. '*Arf, arf!*' he coughed. But his face glowed with pride and pleasure.

I wonder, he thought. I wonder. Did Jack Dash deliberately leave the pot behind as something to remember him by? Did he leave it especially for *me*? thought Maggot. Perhaps, before his human brain finally shut down, Jack had had time for one last generous act?

Maggot would never know for sure. But he really wanted it to be true. He made a solemn vow. I shall treasure this spitting pot all my life. I shall use it always.

He added, And no one else shall be allowed to use it but me. Not even Spud.

Then he put the lid on and stashed the spitting pot safely away in his baggies.

Gran locked the gate. And they cycled off, leaving the mushroom farm behind. It was getting dark. They could see weird lights criss-crossing the pea fields. That was the pea-harvesting machines; they would be working on through the night.

For a long time, neither of them spoke. And then Maggot said, 'Gran?'

'Yes?'

'What was it like being a mushroom?'

Gran pedalled slowly. For a long time, she didn't answer. She was giving Maggot's question some serious thought. Then she said, 'It was really strange. At first, I tried to fight it. But that didn't last long. And after that, I can't remember much. Except,' and here Gran pedalled even more slowly, 'I had these pictures in my head –'

Maggot, who was cycling beside her, was remembering things too. From that brief, confused time – how long had it been? Seconds? Minutes? – *after* he'd breathed in the spores, but *before* the green tea kicked in and clobbered them. Gosh, those spores had worked quickly on him. Much quicker than they did on Gran. Maybe they infected kids' brains much faster.

'What pictures did you see?' Maggot asked Gran nervously.

Gran seemed to be having trouble remembering. Or perhaps she didn't want to.

At last, she said, 'I saw the Earth, my flower. And *we* were everywhere! Some of us were massive, bigger than the post office tower! And I remember feeling really happy. I thought, how beautiful! That's how the world should be. There was no traffic noise, no fighting, no wars. It was so peaceful, with nobody here but us mushrooms. A little *KERRAK!* every now and again, that's all.'

'You were being brainwashed, Gran,' said Maggot gently. 'Mushrooms are really sneaky, you said so yourself. You wouldn't have been one big happy family.'

But Gran wasn't even listening.

Maggot frowned as they cycled along. It sounded suspiciously like Gran quite missed being a mushroom. It didn't surprise him all that much. He'd missed his fungus family too. Just for a short while. He remembered it now – how forlorn and empty he'd felt. As if his life had no meaning without them.

'You've still got me, Gran! And Mum and Dad and Nigel. I know we're only human. But you ought to hear Nigel play his trumpet,' said Maggot, desperately trying to make *normal* conversation. 'He's really improving.'

Maggot gave up. Gran didn't seem interested in the normal world.

He still wasn't too worried. He reasoned, I got over it. Gran will get over it too. But she was infected for much longer than me. So it'll just take her longer to recover.

'Drink loads of that green tea,' Maggot

told Gran. 'Then you'll soon be back to your old self!'

But Gran said nothing. She was silent as a mushroom.

Above their heads, something was riding on the warm breeze, over the pea fields. Maggot and Gran couldn't see it of course. You'd have needed a microscope to do that. But it was a single super-mushroom spore. It had escaped from the fire. It had been hiding in a crack in a bit of charred wood. But then the wind had tugged it free and it had set out on its journey.

The wind blew it this way and that. It blew up the nose of a dad washing his car. But, before he could breathe it in, he sneezed it out again.

It blew to Maggot's town. It couldn't grow just anywhere. It needed a dark secret place it could creep into. Preferably somewhere a bit damp that smelled of mould.

It flew through Nigel's bedroom window and under his bed. No luck there. If it had blown under Maggot's bed, conditions would have been perfect. It would have felt right at home. That furry green pizza slice would have suited it just fine. Or those screwed-up and slightly damp boxer shorts that had been there since Christmas. But Nigel was a neat and tidy-minded person. The space under his bed was just a space. The super-fungus spore carried on searching.

At last it drifted through the ventilation grill of a building. The building was empty, except for a caretaker.

But even if it had been full of children, no one would have seen the spore as it wafted along a corridor.

Just at the right moment, the caretaker was opening a store-room door. The spore floated through and finally landed.

The caretaker locked the store-room door, put the key in his pocket and went away.

The spore landed in the darkness on a pile of straw mats. The mats were right at the back of the store-room. They'd been there for a long time. Everyone had forgotten about them. They were a bit damp and mouldy. There were already some tiny brown toadstools trooping across them. Perfect.

Almost immediately, the spore began to grow. Gran had said fungi were sneaky. She said they were fast movers. But the giant super-mushroom was the fastest and sneaki-est fungus of all.

The spore sent out microscopic thread-like roots. They grew all over the mats and through them, until the mats looked as if they were covered with white candyfloss. Then, on one of the roots, a minute blob appeared. Another blob popped up. Then another. They were white at first but they soon turned blood-red. In the dark store-room, at the back of Miss Miller's classroom in Silver Street School, the super-mushroom family silently, stealthily, carried on growing.

Chapter Eleven

'I'm worried about Gran,' Maggot told Jack Dash.

The royal spitting pot was on the floor of his bedroom. '*Ptong!*' went Maggot.

He greeted each new day by taking careful aim at the spitting pot. He'd never missed once. It was his tribute to Jack Dash.

Lately, he'd even taken to telling Jack Dash his problems. Not a real Jack Dash of course. But Jack Dash as Maggot imagined him, in his wild, pee-drinking adventuring days. Before he got fungified and blown sky-high in the mushroom shed.

'Gran's not infected,' explained Maggot. 'Her eyes don't glow in the dark any more.

Her *body*'s recovered. But being a mushroom has messed up her mind.'

At that moment, Nigel passed Maggot's bedroom door. He saw his little bro, sitting on his bed, talking to empty air. He shook his head sadly.

'She sits at home, sighing and staring into space,' Maggot told Jack Dash with a sigh. 'She doesn't even go road racing any more. She keeps saying things like, "Life has no meaning now I'm not a mushroom"!'

Maggot picked up his school backpack. It was the first day of the new term at Silver Street School.

Before he left his bedroom, Maggot had one last '*Pting!*' in the spitting pot and one last word with Jack Dash.

'She'd better sort herself out,' said Maggot. 'Because Mum thinks she's gone senile. She wants Gran putting in an old folks' home!'

Then he put the pot in the side pocket of his backpack and set off.

Spud was waiting at the end of the road. He was carrying a cage. It contained

Horace, the school's ancient, moth-eaten hamster. It had been Spud's turn to keep him alive during the school holidays.

'Hey!' said Maggot.

'Hey!' said Spud.

Maggot was going to say, 'I needed some help! Why didn't you come out to Gran's?' But he was so pleased to see Spud that he immediately decided to forgive him.

Spud put Horace's cage carefully down on the pavement. Maggot solemnly took his chewing gum out his mouth and parked it behind his ear.

'Ready?'

'Ready.'

They sprang at each other like velociraptors and had a fast, furious fun-fight to show they were still best friends. After all, they hadn't seen each other for two whole weeks. When Maggot came back from Gran's, Spud was away at *his* grandma's. He'd only got back last night.

'Spud,' said Maggot, staggering to his feet. 'No, no, stop fighting for a sec, I'm puffed out. Just listen to this joke. There were two cows in a field. Right? And one says to the other, "Moo!" and the other one says, "Hey, I was going to say that!" Now do you think that's funny?'

Spud laughed, '*Haw, haw, haw!*' so loudly, he scared the crows off the chimney pots. He clutched his stomach. He clung helplessly to a lamp post. Then he fell down, rolled on the ground and kicked his legs in the air. '*Haw! Haw! Haw!*'

Finally he gasped his reply. 'Yes,' he said.

'*Phew,*' said Maggot, relieved. 'I knew *you*'d think it was funny. It's just my mum,' he explained. 'She's got no sense of humour.'

Spud picked up Horace and they carried on walking. In his own good time, Maggot would tell his best friend everything that had happened. About Jack Dash and the giant super-mushrooms and all the rest of it. But he just couldn't face it on the first day of term.

'I'd better take Horace straight into school,' said Spud.

None of their friends were there yet, only some keen infant kids, vrooming around the yard, playing aeroplanes. Maggot and Spud ignored them. They went straight into the building. They were heading for Miss Miller's classroom. It felt strange, going into school early on the first day back. It was eerily quiet. The floors were slippery and smelled of fresh wax.

'Where's Miss Miller?' asked Spud, as he closed the door behind them and looked round the empty classroom.

Maggot shrugged, 'Dunno. Maybe she's not here yet. Maybe she's in the staff room having a cup of tea.'

'Maybe she's in there,' suggested Spud, nodding towards the store-room. There was a key in the door as if somebody was inside.

He put Horace down on Miss Miller's desk. 'I'll just check,' he said.

And he disappeared into the store-room. He left the door half open. Maggot's nose wrinkled. He could smell something foul. It seemed familiar. What could it be?

But his attention was distracted. 'Hiya, Horace!' he said.

Horace had tottered out of his nest for a

quick sip from his water bottle. He creaked round in his wheel once, then gave up. His eyes were tight shut; he wasn't properly awake.

A voice came from deep in the store-room.

'Hey, Maggot! I've found something really gross growing in here. *Yurgh!* They're like big, red brains. One's enormous and, guess what? It's –'

With one bound, Maggot had reached the door. Too late.

KERRAK!

Maggot had to think fast. He hardly hesitated. He slammed the door shut with Spud still inside. He locked it and slipped the key in his pocket. He ripped the gum from behind his ear and plugged the keyhole so no spores could escape.

'Hey,' came Spud's muffled voice from inside. 'What's going on? Stop messing about, Maggot. Let me out! It's all foggy in here!'

KERRAK!

Maggot's heart was tearing in two. But he

had to do the right thing. He had to sacrifice Spud to save the other kids. Soon, they would come trooping into school. A whole schoolful of kids who glowed in the dark and thought they were mushrooms! Not to mention a staff room of fungified teachers. Maggot couldn't bear to think about it. It was too gruesome. But he couldn't bear, either, to leave Spud at the mercy of the giant super-mushrooms. Spud was his best mate – the only person who laughed at his jokes.

Maggot hammered desperately on the door. He yelled through it, 'Spud, can you hear me?'

No reply. The spores were already doing their dirty work, infecting Spud's brain. He was already changing. Soon he would hate the light. His eyes would be zombie eyes. He would breathe cold mushroom breath. He would see Maggot as his deadliest enemy instead of as his closest friend.

Maggot thought of poor Jack Dash in the last stages – a white, rubbery wreck, leaving spore-prints wherever he crawled.

He yelled again through the door. 'I'll come back, Spud. I'll save you. You'll only get a tiny bit fungified. I promise!'

There was only silence from inside the room. The silence of mushrooms.

Maggot frantically looked out of the classroom window. There was Katriona's mum dropping her off at the school gates. And Maggot knew Katriona always had a mobile phone in her backpack.

He skidded towards the classroom door, dived out, clashed it shut behind him. And crashed right into Miss Miller.

'*Aargh!*' Maggot cowered back against the wall, trembling.

Miss Miller looked at him, astonished. She didn't usually scare pupils this much. This child was actually quaking with fear!

'Timothy? What on earth is the matter?'

Maggot checked her eyes. They were still gooseberry green. She hadn't been infected.

'*Phew!*' Maggot wiped his forehead. Then he sprang into the doorway, stretched out his arms and barred her way into the classroom with his body.

Miss Miller looked even more amazed. 'Timothy,' she said. 'I'd like to go into my classroom. I was just going to get some paper from the store-room when I was called away. I'd like to get it out now.'

'Er, no, no offence, miss, but you can't,' gabbled Maggot in a frenzy. 'You can't go in there!'

Miss Miller raised her eyebrows in disbelief. 'Do I understand you correctly, Timothy?' she said. 'Are you saying I cannot enter *my own* classroom?'

'*Arf, arf, arf,*' Maggot did his seal barking act. He was squirming with panic and embarrassment.

'Timothy,' said Miss Miller, tapping her leather sandal in a threatening manner. 'What's going on? Get out of my way. I'd like to go in there NOW.'

Brring! Brring!

That was first bell. It meant ten minutes to go before school started.

'I'd better go to assembly,' said Miss Miller, checking her watch. 'I shall sort this out later!' And she shot one more puzzled look over her shoulder as she hurried away.

'Thank you, thank you, thank you,' gibbered Maggot as he galloped across the school yard. Who was he thanking? He was thanking Jack Dash. In a strange kind of way, Maggot had come to think of Jack Dash as his guardian angel.

'Katriona,' begged Maggot. 'Let me use your mobile, please, please, please. I've got to call Gran.'

Katriona swung her long hair and turned her back on him. 'No one can use it but me,' she said. 'It's not allowed.'

'I won't be a minute. Please, it's a matter of life and death!'

'You're pulling my leg.'

'Honestly, it really is. I can't explain now. Spud's in danger!'

'*Hum*,' Katriona sounded dubious. She was sure he was exaggerating. But she handed the phone over.

Maggot punched in Gran's number. The phone rang and rang. 'Come on, come on,' fretted Maggot.

He willed Gran to answer. But he wasn't

certain she would. Ever since she'd stopped being a mushroom, Gran had been in a world of her own. Some days, she didn't even get out of bed.

At last, a melancholy voice said, 'Who's that?'

'Gran!' shouted Maggot urgently down the phone. 'I need you. It's happened again! You've got to come quick. You've got to bring some green tea!'

'Is that you, my flower?' asked Gran, still sounding terribly dreary, as if all her energy and enthusiasm had been sucked out of her.

'Yes, yes. You've got to come *now*, Gran. The giant super-mushrooms are growing in the school store-room. And Spud's in there with them! He's getting fungified! It works fast on kids. He's probably a mushroom already!'

'Well, worse things happen at sea,' said Gran dreamily. 'Ah, what golden days, when I was a mushroom. We were just one big happy family.'

Maggot danced around with frustration, the phone rammed against his ear. 'No offence, Gran, but that's a load of old twaddle!'

Gran gave a long wistful sigh, as if she was thinking of things that might have been.

Maggot decided to get tough. 'Look, Gran, you've got to face reality! I never told you about the last stage of fungification, did I? Well, it's not pretty! You would have withered up, like a wrinkly old puffball. And you would have been blown away! Just blown away in the wind and forgotten. Jack Dash knew what was going to happen to him. That's why he crawled back into that shed. Cos he was a proper hero. He wanted to go out with a bang. Not blown along in the gutter like some crushed-up, crinkly old crisp packet!'

Maggot made one last desperate appeal. 'We can't let the super-mushrooms win, Gran. We've got to fight them, for Jack Dash's sake. You remember him, don't you? Jack Dash? He was nearly my new grandpa.'

Maggot stopped to listen. But there was no answer from Gran. He let his head droop, hopelessly. He suddenly felt bone-weary, totally drained by his long, heartfelt speech.

'Can I have my phone now?' said Katriona.

He was going to hand it back. But something he said had got through because, suddenly, Gran was speaking to him. There was a shade of the old steel in her voice.

'What did Jack say,' she demanded, 'before he went back into that shed? You lied to me, didn't you, flower? I *knew* he said something.'

Maggot hadn't meant to tell Gran about Jack's last flash of human intelligence. He thought it would be kinder to keep it a secret. But this was an emergency. There wasn't a second to waste. He needed to shock Gran back into the real world. So he told her.

'Jack said, "It's too late for me. Too late!"'

There was a long silence on the other end of the line.

When Gran finally spoke she sounded fierce and determined. As if she'd found a purpose in life again. She said: 'You're right, my flower. That super-mushroom family needs wiping off the face of the Earth.'

She's back to her old self! thought Maggot, almost sobbing with joy.

Brringg! That was the bell for start of school.

'Give – me – my – mobile!' squawked Katriona, trying to snatch it back.

'Wait, wait. Gran are you still there?'

Gran's voice came crackling down the phone.

'I'm on my way!'

'Are you catching the bus into town?' asked Maggot.

'What, are you joking? There isn't one until next Tuesday. I'll just hop on my racing bike. And I'll bring all the green tea I've got!'

Chapter Twelve

Maggot couldn't keep still. He chewed his nails. He checked his watch. He paced restlessly to the window and stared out. He squashed his ear against the store-room door, trying to hear what was going on inside.

'Spud?' he called, tapping on the door. But there was no reply.

He daren't shout too loud. He wasn't supposed to be in the classroom at all. Everyone else was in the school hall, at the long assembly they always had at the start of each new term.

It had been over half an hour since he'd phoned Gran. It took her twenty-five minutes to bike into town with the wind behind her.

She should be here anytime NOW! thought Maggot, checking his watch again.

Right on cue, Gran came speeding into the playground. She was in full road-racing kit: skintight shorts, vest and strawberry helmet. She had a bulging bumbag. And a strange contraption on her back – a blue plastic container with a lever on one side and a hose coming out of the top.

'Gran!' Maggot hissed as he opened the classroom window, 'Climb in here. Don't go through the main doors. They'll see you.'

Gran hauled herself over the windowsill. She had a war-like glint in her eyes.

'OK, my flower,' she said, 'let's get to work! Let's terminate those mushrooms! Let's blast them into oblivion!'

'Hip, hip, hip, hurray!' wafted from the school hall.

'Oh no! They're singing "The Sun Has Got His Hat On"' said Maggot frantically. 'That means Assembly is nearly over.'

Soon Miss Miller and thirty children would come bursting into the room.

'Spud's in there,' said Maggot, pointing to

the store-room door. 'We haven't got much time!'

'No problem.' Gran strode on wiry cycling legs across the classroom. Her lycra racing kit glittered: bright orange, yellow and gold. She looked splendid. Like a rather wrinkly warrior princess. She was in fighting form.

If I was a mushroom, thought Maggot, she'd frighten the life out of me.

'What's that thing on your back?' he asked her.

'The sprayer that I use for my roses. It's full of green tea – industrial strength. Over one hundred times as strong as usual! It'd blow your socks off if you tried to drink it! But it should sort those mushrooms out!

'Here!' said Gran, unzipping her bumbag in one swift movement and thrusting a bottle at Maggot. 'That's the weak stuff for us humans.'

Through the glass, the tea glowed, neon-green, full of swirling things he didn't want to identify.

'Have a swig. But leave some for Spud.'

'What about you?'

'I've had some.'

Maggot tipped up the bottle. Something slippery slid between his teeth. But he was so worked up, he gulped it down. He even forgot to shudder.

'Key?' demanded Gran, holding out her hand.

'Here!' said Maggot, rushing to give it to her. Gran prised the chewing gum out of the lock. 'Good thinking, my flower,' she snapped over her shoulder at Maggot. Maggot blushed pale pink with pride.

'Right!' said Gran. She pointed the hose and started pumping the lever with her elbow.

'Stand clear,' she told Maggot. 'I'm going in!'

'I'm coming too. My mate Spud's in there!'

'No!' ordered Gran, pushing him roughly aside. 'Leave this to me. This is something I've got to do on my own. This is for Jack Dash!'

'Wow!' Maggot breathed in admiration. 'How cool is that?'

Gran slid through the door, quick as a lizard, so no spores could leak out. Maggot caught a brief glimpse of something monstrous, blood-red and bulging. It seemed to fill the store-room.

'Watch yourself!' Maggot warned Gran. 'Spud'll try to protect the super-mushrooms. He's usually rubbish at fighting. But now he's got a mushroom's strength!'

But the door had already slammed shut behind her.

Maggot could hardly bear the terrible tension.

His eyes were glued to the store-room door. But he couldn't hear anything – that was the most agonising thing. There was a massive fight going on in there. Gran and the green tea versus Spud and the super-mushrooms. But it was happening in creepy silence. He hadn't a clue who was winning.

He couldn't stand it a second longer. He had to ignore Gran's orders.

'I can't just *wait*. I've got to help her!'

Then a puddle spread out from under the door. It was deep emerald green. Maggot watched it, fascinated, as it flowed towards him. It swilled round his trainers. They soaked it up like a sponge.

'*Ugh!*' said Maggot, paddling to a bit of dry floor.

Then an even more sinister substance leaked out. It didn't gush under the door. It slithered. It was thick and sticky like tar. And it gave off a powerful smell – of dead and decaying mushrooms. A solitary bluebottle came zooming in through the open classroom window.

Spud's dissolved into black slime! thought Maggot hysterically.

Then the store-room door burst wide open. *Bang!* It crashed into the wall. The sudden noise, after all that silence, made Maggot's heart leap like a frog.

Spud staggered out. He was still in one piece. He hadn't dissolved. But, as Maggot expected, he was partly fungified. His mushroom eyes were like milky marbles.

'Spud! You've got to drink this!'

Maggot threw himself on his friend. It was like one of their biggest fun fights. Only this time it wasn't a joke. This time it was deadly serious.

'Drink it!' panted Maggot, trying to wrestle Spud and unscrew the bottle with his teeth.

Spud had never been a muscle man. He had trouble ripping open an ice pop. But being fungified made him strong. He fought like a demon.

As they struggled on the floor, Maggot heard the cheery strains of 'The Sun Has Got His Hat On'. This was the seventeenth time they'd practised the same verse! Surely they'd get it right soon.

And then they'll all come racing back here! Maggot thought desperately.

Panic gave him more than mushroom strength. He held Spud down and emptied most of the bottle of green tea between his teeth.

Glug, glug, glug. Was that an African centipede Spud had just swallowed? Or a millipede? It slid down too quickly for Maggot to count its legs.

Spud had stopped fighting now. He'd

calmed down. He was gurgling a lot though. Trickles of green tea were running down his chin. Maggot left him on the floor to recover and concentrated on the open store-room door. Gran was backing out slowly, squelching through black goo, her sprayer still trained on something inside.

Maggot got up. His legs suddenly felt wobbly. He had to hang on to Miss Miller's desk.

'That's got rid of that,' said Gran grimly.

Maggot stared into the store-room. Green tea dripped from the walls and ceiling. The super-mushrooms had melted into smelly black sludge.

'Hey!' said Maggot, slapping Gran on the back. 'I thought those mushrooms were unstoppable. But the green tea zapped them. Look what it did! It just dissolved them. Easy-peasy!' He was wild with relief and happiness.

'*Humm*,' said Gran thoughtfully. She wasn't celebrating. She had a troubled look on her face. 'Almost too easy,' she said. She looked round the classroom. 'Survival of the spores. That's what it's all about.'

'Well, everything's all right. None escaped did they?'

'My flower,' said Gran, 'you've forgotten one of the main characteristics of mushrooms. They're sneaky. Very, very sneaky.'

But Maggot wasn't listening. He was kneeling beside Spud. 'Spud!' he told him joyfully. 'Everything's all right! The green tea saved you. You're not a mushroom any more! And the giant super-mushrooms are DEAD!'

Spud looked totally baffled. 'Actually,' he said in a dazed voice, 'I quite like mushrooms.'

Oh no, thought Maggot with sudden dread. Anxiously, he shook Spud's arm. 'Concentrate, Spud!' he said. 'I'm going to ask you a very important question. Does your life have no meaning now that you're not a mushroom?'

'No way!' Spud cried, in a wounded voice. 'My life has lots of meaning. Look, I'm re-growing this scab on my elbow so I can pick it off again. And I'm practising standing on one leg for three minutes without wobbling.

And I'm trying to suck a Polo mint until it's really, *really* thin before it breaks.'

'Just checking,' said Maggot. 'But I thought you said you liked mushrooms.'

'Well, I do. I love 'em. On top of a pizza, with pepperoni.'

'I'd better make myself scarce,' said Gran, shutting the store-room door. 'And you two, you'd better go back where you ought to be, pronto. If they find us here,' and her eyes darted to the sticky green and black pools on the floor, 'we're going to have a lot of explaining to do.'

Maggot and Spud slipped into Assembly through a back door and mingled with the crowd. Just in time to sing, 'HIP, HIP, HIP, HURRAY!' ten times louder than anyone else. They looked a bit the worse for wear. Spud had a mystified frown on his face. And they both looked as if they'd been slime-bombed. But none of their teachers noticed anything unusual about them.

Meanwhile, Gran was cycling back through the pea fields. It was a beautiful morning, cloudless, serene. Her victory over the super-mushrooms should have made her sing out loud too. But *she* wasn't belting out any cheery tunes. Instead, she was humming to herself – very, very thoughtfully.

Back on Miss Miller's desk, Horace, the ancient hamster, seemed to have got a new lease of life. His wheel was going round at warp speed! He braked it with a shower of sparks, then sprang to the bars and gazed murderously round the classroom with white, glowing, mushroom eyes.

Chapter Thirteen

That evening, after school, Maggot cycled out to Gran's house. He had something very important to tell her.

'Gran!' he shouted, crashing through the door.

Gran wasn't in the kitchen. He went upstairs and there she was, in her bedroom, trying on an amazing pair of shorts.

They were khaki-coloured and baggy, even baggier than Maggot's pants. And they bristled with zipped pockets, like rows of snarling silver teeth.

'They're my trekking shorts,' explained Gran. 'Look at all these really useful pockets. Only trouble is, I keep forgetting which pocket I've put things in.'

'You're not going away, are you?' said Maggot, dismayed. 'Where are you trekking to?'

'To the jungle, of course,' said Gran. 'I'm following in Jack's footsteps. I'm going to try and get hold of some more of that green tea. I've nearly run out. And we've got to be ready. We may need *lots* more.'

'That's what I came to tell you,' interrupted Maggot. 'The spores escaped. At least, some of them did. Horace the hamster breathed them in. His eyes were like little laser beams! He was bending the bars of his cage with one paw!'

'What did you do?'

'It was tricky, Gran. Miss Miller and the caretaker were going bananas because of the mess on the floor. And they hadn't even looked in the store-room yet! Anyway, there was a little bit of tea left in the bottle I gave to Spud. So I sneaked up and filled Horace's water bottle with it. But Miss Miller saw me. She said, "Are you trying to poison Horace? Why is his drinking water bright green?"'

'Oh no, what did you tell her?'

'I told her it was a spinach tonic, specially recommended for hamsters.'

'She didn't believe that, did she?'

'Yes, she did,' said Maggot, shaking his head in amazement. 'I don't think teachers get out much. I used to think, when I was little, that they lived in school cupboards.'

'Anyway, you cured him?' said Gran.

'Yep, he's back to his crumbly old self.'

He could hardly bear to think of the consequences if he hadn't been able to cure Horace. He would have become a tiny furry fungus on four legs. Then died, a shrivelled shell.

'Poor old hammy,' said Gran, as if she was reading Maggot's mind. 'He might have been better off as a mushroom. At least he'd be in a crowd. It's a lonely life being a hamster, stuck on your own in a cage.'

'Gran!' said Maggot, alarm bells ringing in his brain. 'You don't really think that!'

'Don't worry,' said Gran. 'I'm not still under the spell of the giant super-mushrooms. But I remember how powerful those mushroom dreams can be. So do you, don't you?'

Maggot frowned and nodded.

'And we're the only two people who know about it. At least, the only two people left alive,' said Gran, looking sad for a second. 'Except for your friend Spud of course. Have you told him the whole story yet?'

'*Arf, arf,*' barked Maggot, embarrassed. 'No, actually, I haven't, Gran. I will, I will honest. Except that I don't know where to start. It's sort of complicated, isn't it?'

'You're not kidding,' agreed Gran. 'But it's even more complicated than you think. Sit down for a minute.'

Maggot sat down on Gran's bed. He felt that there was bad news coming.

'Mushrooms,' Gran told him, 'must never be underestimated. Jack Dash told me that. They're the oldest living organisms on Earth. Did you know that? Just think what they've seen! And just think about this,' Gran said. 'Their spores send down these little roots called hyphae. And, if conditions are right, they can spread miles and miles

145

underground. They can live, secretly, in the soil for years. And every so often a mushroom comes popping up. But when it dies, it doesn't mean the whole fungus is dead. Oh no. It means the hyphae are spreading underground in darkness. Just waiting.'

Maggot shivered. 'I knew they were sneaky,' he said, appalled. 'But I never knew they were that sneaky! Does that mean the hyphae are spreading underground from Silver Street School. Even though you zapped the top bit?'

'I don't think so,' said Gran. 'I checked. That floor under the store-room is thick concrete. The giant super-mushrooms could've cracked it and spread underground – eventually. But I think we were lucky. We caught it just in time. We've still got the spores to worry about though. There may be more drifting round your school. Horace might not have breathed them all in.'

'I've been wondering about that,' said Maggot. 'I think we were lucky there too. No one else in the class got infected. So maybe no more of them escaped.' He really wanted it to be true. After all the tragic things that had been happening, they deserved a bit of good luck.

'Maybe you're right,' agreed Gran. 'But we can't take the chance. If those super-mushrooms break out again and start fungifying people, we've got to be prepared! When I come back with the green tea, I'll get you one of those backpack sprays. We can work as a team.'

Gran's eyes were shining with new purpose. She had a mission in life again. She had filled that big gap that was left when she stopped being a mushroom.

'Mushroom busters!' said Maggot. 'People will call us the mushroom busters!'

'I don't care what they call us,' said Gran. 'As long as those blasted super-mushrooms don't take over the world. By the way, I just thought about something. There weren't any baby super-mushrooms growing in Horace's cage were there? I mean, those are ideal conditions! All that damp smelly straw and endless supplies of hamster poo! They'd just love it.'

'I've already thought of that,' interrupted Maggot hastily.

He felt that he was getting to know the habits of the giant super-mushrooms, anticipating their wily ways. 'I cleaned the cage and chucked out the old straw and sawdust. I didn't see anything growing in there. And I had a really good sort through. It was just before I ate my packed lunch.'

'Well done, my flower,' said Gran. 'You've got to stay one step ahead of these mushrooms. Jack Dash would have been proud of you.'

'Do you think so?' said Maggot, with a grin of pure delight.

'I know so,' said Gran firmly.

'I wish I could come with you, Gran,' said Maggot. 'Go to the same places he went – where he did his fungus hunting and lion-wrestling. And meet the people who made him a prince.'

'Not this time,' said Gran. 'I'll send you postcards. And, in any case,' she said folding up a mosquito net. 'It'll be a short trip. I'm not hanging around. I plan to trade for the green tea – and get back as soon as possible.'

'What are you going to trade,' said Maggot. 'Beads and things?'

'For heaven's sake,' said Gran. 'People don't want beads these days. Where did you get that idea? No, I'll be taking out some designer jeans and clockwork radios. Which reminds me,' said Gran, 'now I'm on the subject of trousers. Have you got that royal spitting pot in your baggies?'

'Yes, I have!' said Maggot protectively. 'I carry it with me always! I made a solemn vow.'

'Can I borrow it?' asked Gran. 'I promise I'll look after it. But I need some form of identification. To show Jack's friends that I really knew him.'

'Well, all right,' said Maggot reluctantly, pulling out the small silver spitting pot and putting it on Gran's bedside table. 'But don't spit in it, will you? Only I'm allowed to do that.'

'I'll treat it very respectfully,' said Gran. 'In memory of Jack.'

'In memory of Jack,' agreed Maggot solemnly.

And, for a moment, they were silent. Both of them had Jack Dash on their minds. Usually, Maggot pictured Jack in his wild, pee-drinking days. Before the super-mushrooms destroyed him. But this time he saw him crawling back into the blazing shed in his mildewed top hat and wedding suit. *Jingle, jingle*. He could almost hear those bottle-tops clinking around Jack's neck.

He was a hero to the end, thought Maggot, with a brave, sad smile.

Maggot was the first to speak.

'Gran,' he said. 'I've got something to show you.' He started peeling off his sock. He separated his big toe from the next one. Gran peered at his foot. She put on her reading glasses. 'I can't see anything.'

'Exactly!' said Maggot triumphantly. 'There's one *good* thing about all this. That mega-strong green tea this morning – I was paddling in it and it soaked through my trainers and socks. I had soggy feet all day. But look at this. When I took my socks off, hey presto, I couldn't believe it. My foot fungus was completely gone!'

Chapter Fourteen

Maggot was right about the spores from the store-room. The only ones that escaped had been snuffled up by Horace the hamster and then killed by the green tea. There was nothing to fear from them.

And Gran was right too, about the hyphae in the store-room. They had burrowed through the pile of straw mats. But they hadn't had time to sneak through the concrete and take cover underground. They had ended up, just like the fruiting bodies of the giant super-mushroom, sprayed into sticky black slime.

But both the mushroom busters missed something. It happened out in the pea fields – on the very day Gran returned with fresh supplies of green tea and a bottle-top necklace honouring her as a tribal princess.

The great red pea-harvesters were trundling across the landscape. On the horizon was Jack Dash's mushroom farm. It was locked up and deserted. Nothing had been touched since the day of the fire. Jack's 'MUSHROOMS R ME' van was still parked there. There was still a black hole in the ground where the mushroom shed had exploded.

Suddenly, out in the pea fields, one of the red machines jerked to a halt. The driver climbed down from his cab.

What on earth's that? he thought.

Among the waist-high green plants, something was hiding. Hyphae, that had travelled underground for two miles, had sent it up into the daylight. The hyphae had found it easy to burrow through the soil floor of the shed. They had been growing underground for some time. On the day of the big fire, Maggot thought the giant super-mushrooms had been totally fried. What he didn't know was that, right under his feet, a network of hyphae had escaped from the mushroom farm. They had spread under the wire fence days ago and were already heading towards the pea fields.

The driver whistled in amazement. He parted the pea plants. He knelt down to take a closer look.

It was as big as a small child, deep red and egg-shaped. It had a surface like raw steak, but crinkled and tucked into folds.

It stank of mould and decay.

The driver prodded it. '*Ugh!*' The thing looked swollen and puffed-up. As if it was ripe and ready to burst. Where he poked it, the flesh oozed red juice and turned navy blue like a bruise.

He felt scared and revolted. He made a sudden decision. He was all alone. The nearest pea harvester was just a red splodge in the distance. There was no one else around.

'I'll drive over it!' he said, thinking out loud. 'I'll smash it into pulp.'

He was climbing back into his cab when a strange noise, sharp as a whip crack, made him turn round.

KERRAK!